The Water Tree Way

The Water Tree Way

Ruth Mendelson

The Water Tree Way

Contact the author: ruth@ruthmendelson.com

Contact the publisher: info@thewatertreeway.com

Cover design: Arch Apolar

ISBN: 978-1-7361970-0-4

First Edition

This is a work of fiction. Any resemblances to actual persons, living or dead, events, businesses, or places are purely coincidental and products of the author's imagination.

FOR EVERYONE EVERYWHERE.

ESPECIALLY YOU.

TABLE OF CONTENTS

FOREWORD

Dr. Jane Goodall DBE

Books have been a part of my life since I was a little girl. They helped fuel my dreams—dreams that would ultimately lead me on an adventure to Africa where I would spend many years studying and working with all sorts of extraordinary animals— mostly, of course, the chimpanzees.

I originally met Ruth, the author of *The Water Tree Way*, at the UN in Geneva, Switzerland in 2002, where she was opening as a musician for an international peace summit. We became fast friends. Over the years we have embarked on a number of wonderful creative collaborations, including recording the updated audio version of my book, *My Life with the Chimpanzees* (Hatchet Press). It was a memorable occasion—in forty-five minutes flat, Ruth and her engineer converted my small hotel room into a studio that would ensure my voice was recorded at a professional quality. Surrounded by the mountains of hotel pillows and blankets kindly provided by the staff to filter out sounds from the hallway, Ruth and I, together with the sound engineer, sat for hours as I recorded the narration for the book. What makes this audio version so special is the soundtrack she and her team created using the authentic sounds of the forest—

insects, birds, gurgling streams, wind, rain and, of course, chimpanzees.

Sometime later, Ruth sent me an electronic version of her own book and asked if I would consider writing an introduction. Prior to reading it, I had only known her as a talented musician, teacher, film composer and humanitarian. After reading *The Water Tree Way*, I am delighted to introduce this enchanting story to you. It will appeal to the child in us all. And adults will quickly notice the valuable hidden messages in each chapter.

The heroine Jai (pronounced Jay) is a young girl whose name means "Victory." As we start reading, Jai's life seems similar to that of many children. We soon learn that she has a life-long dream to go on a "Great Adventure"—an idea so improbable and daring that only one of her friends could even consider joining her. But Jai must set out on her own.

She is exhilarated, yet soon finds that her path is not easy. Jai learns many lessons as she faces challenges and survives the many sometimes frightening experiences along the way. She learns to be patient and persistent and that she has a courage she did not know she possessed.

And she learns to value the help and advice of the magical cast of characters who both protect her from peril and guide her through the sometimes-hilarious buffoonery of her own mistakes.

In a subtle way, the lessons Jai learns will help readers to overcome some of the problems they may face in their families and schools. There are lessons for us all about the need to protect the environment and the folly of much human conflict.

But the overriding message concerns the resilience of the human spirit, the importance of understanding how all life is interconnected. The importance of not always taking things at face value.

As Jai continues on her journey, she learns of an inner music that reverberates throughout time and space. This music is sending a message not only to her, but to the entire world if we would only listen. The music of the stars is always available, energizing us and bringing a sense of peace. Deep reverberation of drums appear and vanish throughout the story, beckoning Jai—and us—to action. Most of the adults in Jai's world are deaf to this music and have forgotten their own "Great Adventures." They no longer believe that the ancient Water Trees, which grow by the river at the edge of town, are there to assist them. But the children know.

Each and every one of us can be inspired by Jai's example. Take some quiet time to reflect on the rare and valuable gifts and talents within each of us. Most of us have a dream, sometimes buried so deep within the humdrum tedium of daily life that we have forgotten it. Attune your ears to the music of the stars and understand that it is telling you to follow your heart.

Remember that every day, each one of us makes a difference on our planet, and we can choose what sort of difference we make. In today's world, more than ever, we need people who make honest and ethical choices. We need you.

~ Dr. Jane Goodall DBE

The Water Tree Way

CHAPTER 1

Jai bit her lip and hoisted herself up onto the plank. Her knees wobbled slightly as she inched her way towards the edge of the diving board. She'd never attempted anything this bold in all her life. Sure, last summer she had lunged into the swimming pool from the low board, but THIS was the *Nose-Bleed Section;* the highest dive at the town pool. She had always wanted to try it, and besides that, she was ten years old and getting ready to go on a Great Adventure. The Water Trees told her the time was coming, and they know everything.

Her body teetered as she struggled to adjust to the height.

"Hey you guys, it's WINDY up here!"

Jai peered down at her friends below. Billy, her *most* trusted friend, offered an encouraging thumbs up with his regular athletic ease. His uncombed mop of thick brown hair was easy to spot from all the way up there. Natalie Snoot scurried from the pool's edge. She'd do *anything* to avoid getting her new hair-do wet. Meanwhile, Michael Peabody III adjusted his glasses, anticipating the thrill of a death-defying dive. As the class brain, he pondered what Jai's total velocity might be when she hit the water. Others kids continued to gather around the pool's edge. Most wondered if she'd actually have the guts to go through with it—hardly *anybody* ever went all the way up there.

Jai's ears popped from the altitude. Everyone looked so small from this height. Staring beyond her bare feet on the board, she froze. She wasn't expecting to feel so afraid. She was not a stranger to fear, but courage always seemed to follow right behind. Things tended to happen quickly for Jai. She didn't like having to wait for stuff, be it courage or anything else. Regardless, as she stood alone in that moment, bravery was nowhere in sight. Her thoughts drifted to her mother and the last time they had been together at the pool. They had bobbed together playfully in the shallow section, her mother holding her tight. The warmth of her mother's skin was always a happy memory for Jai. But that was a long time ago.

Jai adjusted her swimsuit as the crowd continued to grow. Dax Googan had arrived on the scene, and that always meant trouble.

Snatching a juice box from a younger boy's hands, Dax put the straw to his mouth and took a long, exaggerated sip.

"Thanks for the juice, PIGHEAD!"

The little boy started to cry. Seeing this, Jai's toes clenched in anger. The younger boy was a new kid in town. Everybody knew that.

"Leave him alone, Googan!" The plank bounced slightly as Jai yelled. "Give it back!"

Dax continued sipping the boy's juice, ignoring her.

That did it. Being ignored when you're saying something important is *the worst*. At least according to Jai.

"I said, GIVE IT BACK!"

Forgetting everything, she leapt off the diving board in a fury. Wide-eyed, Dax dropped the juice box and started to run. Jai sailed through the air towards the water, arms flailing. Her chaotic descent ended with an abrupt and painful SPLASH! Truly, it was a belly-flop of epic proportions.

Jai dragged herself out from the pool, clobbered. Her skin sizzled red hot from the unforgiving slap of the water. Without a word, she picked up the juice box and handed it to the boy.

Her friend Billy ran up to her, grinning.

"You okay?"

He'd seen Jai get into mischief a zillion times before— almost as often as him.

Jai shot a pained glance at the *Nose-Bleed Section* and announced, "I'm done with diving."

As soon as she said it, she knew something wasn't right.

Most people were both puzzled and dazzled by Jai's escapades. She could climb trees faster than any other kid in town, she could spit farther than most boys twice her age (she took great pride in this), and she was the first—and only— person to ever give a concert featuring underwater harmonica (exhaling only). Jai would try just about anything. But her true goal in life was to pluck one of the Leaves that grew from the Water Trees. All of the kids in town loved the mysterious and magical Water Tree Grove that flourished beside the river, near the edge of town. Of course, adults knew about the Grove, but once grown up they seemed to forget the magical powers of the trees and to instead see the grove as merely a favorite play spot.

Jai's name was pronounced "Jay," and it meant *victory*. When she was younger, her father would tell her the story of her name every night before bed. He'd always start out in the same way.

"Years ago, Jai, your mother met a wise woman."

Jai would listen eagerly, her heart thumping in anticipation.

"This wise woman spoke a rare and ancient language. She took a liking to your mom. Everyone did—after all, she was the most beautiful woman in all the world. So as a gift, the wise woman taught your mom a word from her language—"jai"— saying that it carried a special power, and that it meant *victory*. When you were born, we knew from the first time we saw you that your name was to be Jai, because you have that special power. It's right there in your eyes."

Jai's eyes *were* breathtaking. Her deep brown orbs were speckled with small and surprising flecks of bright purple. But you could only see the purple if you really looked.

"You can accomplish anything you set your mind to, Jai. Just like your name says—*Victory!*"

And with that, he would kiss her goodnight.

Jai always felt a little mixed at this point—elated to hear about her mother, but sad to see the droop in her father's lanky body when he rose from the bed. Her mom had been killed when

Jai was just three years old. Ever since then, his body sagged a bit—like a plant that needed water.

"Dad?"

"Yes, Honey."

"Maybe you'll see Mom in a dream tonight!"

Her father would smile sadly.

"Maybe, Pumpkin. You have a good imagination. Now go to sleep. I'll see you in the morning."

Then he would turn off the light, always making sure to leave a night light on in the hallway.

Waiting for sleep wasn't always easy for Jai, but *being* asleep was magical. Deep in the night, her mother would visit her in dreams. They'd play and laugh and talk about all sorts of things. Jai *knew* those visits were real—she was sure of it!

Of all the dreams she'd had with her mother, the most important one happened four years earlier, when Jai was only six years old. That was the dream that changed everything. In it, she and her mother were sitting together on a soft blue blanket atop a hill. The sun had just set and all was quiet. Her mom was gently stroking Jai's hair.

"Watch for the first star, Jai. Can you find it?"

Her mother's eyes sparkled deep brown and purple, just like Jai's, only they were etched with the wisdom that comes from being older.

Jai laid her head in her mother's lap and gazed at the sky. Eventually, a tiny pinhead of light appeared. It twinkled softly and, as if a little shy, began to sing. A pure, sweet melody floated across the entire cosmos, revealing secrets of far-away places and unexplored treasures. It was the most beautiful song Jai had ever heard. Her mother smiled tenderly.

"It will be time soon, Jai. Remember—in taking Great Adventures, you'll find the greatest treasure of all. One of those Water Tree Leaves is meant for you. Do you know which one it is?

"I'm so very proud of you, Jai. We'll all be watching over you."

Her mother gently touched Jai's shirt. It was bright yellow with golden buttons down the front. Jai only wore fancy shirts in dreams. After all, they must cost a lot of money. Her mother noticed that the button at the very bottom was missing.

"Let me show you something, Jai."

She then produced a single golden button and began to teach Jai how to sew it on, explaining how things we learn today can become important for us tomorrow.

And then the dream was over.

Jai shot awake in her bed—thinking about Great Adventures and sewing. In all of her six years, she had never considered sewing to be all that important.

In a flash, she exploded out of bed and ran to the kitchen.

"DAD!"

Her father was sitting at the kitchen table, groggily drinking his morning coffee and reading the newspaper. Jai raced over and gave him a hug.

"Dad! I saw Mom last night!"

Her father paused and stretched.

"That's nice, Honey."

He reached for a box of cereal, prepared a bowl for Jai and resumed reading the paper. She wanted to tell him all about her dream, but his attention was now on the day's weather forecast. He looked tired. Her dad was holding down two jobs and, even though it was a Saturday, he had to leave for work soon.

"Can I go the Water Tree Grove after breakfast?"

"Sure, Honey, just remember to go to Mrs. Grockle's house afterwards. I won't be home 'til late."

Mrs. Grockle was their next-door neighbor. Jai stayed with her when her dad worked weekends.

"Mrs. Grockle? Her cookies taste like cardboard!"

"It won't be forever, Pumpkin. Just 'til I find a better job."

Jai wolfed down her cereal as her father read to her about the weather. She was never interested in this, but her father recited the forecast almost every morning. After a hug and a kiss, they were both out the door. Her dad headed for work in their clunky old car and Jai raced, at full speed, to the Water Tree Grove.

Water Trees were very old and very wise. Everything about them was unique—even their bark. Unlike the rough texture of most trees, Water Tree bark was soft and rolling, a rich blue velvet robe that rippled like water at the slightest touch of the wind.

But what Jai loved most were their Leaves. Each Water Tree produced only one Leaf at a time—never more—with a secret map tucked deep inside. No two maps were alike, yet each one promised a Great Adventure filled with countless riches and magical destinations. There was a catch, however: each map was revealed only *after* the Leaf was plucked (never before), and whoever did the plucking had to go on the map's journey. There was no turning back. Few people had the guts to even touch one of those Leaves, not to mention pluck one.

Jai arrived at the Water Tree Grove, hair windblown from running, and bounded up to the Eldest Tree, who had become like a grandparent to her. She plopped down on the ground before the Tree, panting.

"I had the most amazing dream last night!"

"Ah, sounds like you had a visit from your mother!"

Jai smiled. Water Trees know EVERYTHING!

"What did she tell you, Jai?"

"That one of the Leaves is for me!"

The Eldest Tree looked at her at her with ancient, thoughtful eyes.

"Do you know which one it is?"

"I think so!"

One Leaf in particular had always amazed her. It grew from the lowest branch of the Eldest Tree and seemed to have a life of its own. It would mysteriously change shape from a large blue Leaf, to a bird, and back to a Leaf. Jai sat for hours by the tree, waiting to see what the leaf would do next. One time she saw it morph from a leaf into a swan, then a pelican, and back into a Leaf again. She was utterly mystified.

Reading her thoughts, the Eldest Tree chuckled.

"That Leaf is meant for someone who is especially free-spirited, Jai. Now, this is a big decision and there are many Leaves, so be sure to take a good look at all of your choices before you decide. Take your time."

All of the Water Trees smiled in a gentle, noble sort of way, their soft blue bark rippling in the breeze. Jai walked slowly through the Grove, inspecting each of the Leaves that dangled from their branches. They were all beautiful, all flawless, all rich velvety blue—but her eyes kept returning to the Leaf on the Eldest Tree. It radiated a mysterious glow as it morphed into a perched hawk before slipping back into the shape of a Leaf.

The Eldest Tree smiled.

"Whoever chooses this Leaf must be very strong. Are you sure?"

Jai walked over to it and, without hesitation, reached out to shake hands, so to speak. The Leaf felt surprisingly soft and strong as it sparkled violet blue and bright gold at her touch. Elated, she looked at the Eldest Tree and announced,

"This is the one!"

All of the Water Trees cheered. It wasn't every day that someone had the courage to choose a Leaf. Jai immediately began tugging away, wanting to know more. But no matter how hard she pulled, the Leaf refused to give.

There was a reason for that. In their wisdom, Water Trees would never allow their Leaves to be plucked until the person doing the tugging was strong enough to go on the Leaf's journey. Going on a Great Adventure is a big commitment and one has to be ready.

Jai tried everything to get that Leaf off The Tree. She pulled it, tugged it, yanked it, and even grabbed it and swung from it like a rope. Nothing worked. the Leaf dangled lazily from its branch without a care in the world.

Exhausted, Jai looked to the Eldest Tree.

"What's wrong? Aren't I ready yet?"

"No, Jai. Not yet."

"But I'm already six!"

"The time will come. In the meantime, you must be patient."

She had no choice. The Leaf wouldn't budge.

That was four years ago. Jai was now ten years old and had just performed the worst belly flop in world history. Her hair drenched, her skin still stinging from the crash, Jai stood by the pool with Billy, who was getting restless.

"Hey, let's go to the Water Trees! C'mon Jai, you'll feel better."

Jai didn't answer. She was hungry and preoccupied. It bothered her that after all that time, she had not yet been able to pluck that Leaf yet, and her stomach growled in agreement. She'd been trying to pull that Leaf off every single day since she was six—almost half her life.

"It'll happen, Jai. You know it will."

Billy understood Jai like nobody else (except the Water Trees). After all, they were best friends. An active kid, he always looked like his hair and clothes were trying to catch up with him.

He never tied his gym shoes (unless on the soccer field), never finished tucking in his shirt (a waste of time as far as he was concerned), never combed his hair. Jai was much neater. Her short black hair wisped playfully, and she always tied her shoelaces. Purple high tops were her favorite shoes. She was convinced they helped her run faster.

The two friends walked in silence. Eventually Jai stopped to pick up a stone. Narrowing her eyes, she hurled it at a tin can that had been left on a wooden fence nearby. The can blasted off the ledge as if hit by a comet.

Billy nodded approvingly and Jai's stomach growled in reply.

"Let's go to my house first. My dad made brownies last night."

Now ten years old, she no longer had to go to Mrs. Grockle's house when her dad was at work. Even so, he always left a special snack out on the kitchen table.

Billy's eyes brightened.

"Brownies?! C'mon! Race ya!"

Billy took off in a flash. Jai flew after him yelling.

"You don't even stand a chance!"

The two friends bounded up to Jai's house, pushed each other around at the door before racing into the kitchen and digging into the freshly baked tin of brownies. His cheeks gorged to the max, Billy struggled to speak.

"I think it's gonna to be soon, Jai."

Beyond his garbled, crumb-spewing words, she knew what he meant: The Water Tree Leaf.

Jai's mouth was so stuffed she couldn't talk at all. Eventually she gulped down enough to make room for some words to escape.

"Do you have...*that*...feeling?"

Billy kept chewing and nodded.

"Yup. *That* one."

Billy had a way of knowing things that other people didn't. It had always been that way. And, like Jai, he also dreamt of singing stars. They were the only ones who knew that about each other—except the Water Trees, who know everything anyway.

After their snack, they headed towards the river to The Water Tree Grove, and Jai resumed what had become known at school as *Jai's Leaf Challenge*. Without fail, she spent hours every day trying to pull that Leaf off the Tree—after school, during the summer when it was so hot her hands would slip from all the sweat, during the winter when her fingers were almost frostbitten and burned for hours after she returned home. In all seasons and all weather—Jai could be found at the Grove pulling on that Leaf. Sometimes her classmates would come and place bets on whether this was the Big Day or not.

Strengthened from newly devoured brownies, Jai tugged on the Leaf while Billy practiced spinning a basketball on his finger. Meanwhile, the Eldest Tree watched Jai closely, monitoring her progress.

"That's enough for today," announced The Tree after a while.

"It's not that late!" Jai said, clearly winded. "Can't I try a bit longer?"

"Come back tomorrow—you're much closer than you think. It'll be soon, Jai."

Billy grabbed the twirling ball off his finger. "Soon! I *told ya!*"

Jai released her grip on the Leaf. It morphed into a seagull and gave her a mischievous peck on the head, then immediately turned back into a Leaf.

Jai jumped back, startled.

With a twinkle in its eye, The Elder Tree laughed out loud, repeating, "It'll be soon."

The next day, Jai returned to The Grove by herself. Billy was at soccer practice and would join up later. Her friends had other things to do. She was tugging away at the Leaf when something unusual happened. She could have sworn she heard the small brown Stem whisper something. Curious, Jai put her ear up to the Stem and, to her astonishment, heard a small voice say, "Try harder."

"But I *am* trying!"

"Like that belly flop the other day? Really, Jai, that was horrendous!"

Jai stopped.

"How do you know about that?!"

"How could you just give up like that?"

"I didn't give up! It's not like I climbed back down. I just...landed hard."

This is weird, she thought. She didn't know stems could talk.

"Of course we can talk!" replied the Stem, reading her thoughts. "As for that dive, I'm not talking about the *landing*! C'mon! *THINK!*"

Jai looked blankly at the Stem.

"Honestly, Jai, are you *ever* going to be ready for this?"

"Now, now," interrupted the Eldest Tree gently. "Remember, she's still learning."

Jai scratched her head.

"What does a belly flop have to do with anything? It's simple: I can't dive!"

The Stem gasped. "You used *that* word!"

"But I CAN'T!"

Not knowing what else to do, she pulled harder at the Leaf. It held on stronger than ever, as if cemented on.

In between tugs Jai thought a moment. The Stem was right. She knew better than to use the word "can't." It went against everything her name stood for.

"OK, maybe I need to change my mind on this one."

"Better," noted the Stem, "but I'm still not convinced."

Jai continued tugging at the Leaf, but it refused to be plucked. *The Leaf Challenge* continued with no end in sight. Eventually, the Stem spoke.

"So you want to go on a Great Adventure?"

"Of course I do!"

"Then get back up there."

"Where?"

"On that diving board!"

"WHAT?! I can't do that!"

"There's that word again!"

The Stem refused to say anything else. Even the Water Trees were unusually quiet.

Jai continued tugging on the Leaf. She was frustrated and—even worse—afraid. The thought of that high dive terrified her. She didn't want to go back—period. And yet, deep in her gut, Jai had the uneasy knowing that she had two options. She could return to *The Nose Bleed Section* and try it again, or she could spend the rest of her life in a tug-of-war with a Leaf that would never budge. Summer was almost over and the town pool would be closing soon. School was about to start. With great reluctance, she released the Leaf, left The Grove and headed home for her swimsuit. Jai met Billy who was on his way to meet her at The Grove.

"Where ya goin,' Jai?" he asked.

"I have to get back up there."

Billy nodded. He knew exactly what she was talking about. "Can I come?"

"Sure. But I have to go home and change first."

The walk from her house to the pool seemed longer than usual. Sure—she dreaded the height, the water, the thought of another painful crash, but those weren't her only problems. Jai's belly flop had become legendary across town. Plus, the pool was full of kids trying to squeeze in as much swim-time as possible before it closed for the season. Jai pushed the gate to the pool open with one forceful kick. It made a loud bang against the fence. EVERYONE stopped playing, left the water, and gathered at the edge to see what would happen next.

The only sound that could be heard was the quick flop, flip, flop, flip of Jai's sandals as she made her way to the ladder. Yet, all she could hear was the sound of her heart pounding. She paused at the bottom of the ladder, took a deep breath, placed her right foot onto the first smooth steel rung, and carefully made her way back up to *The Nose Bleed Section*. The air felt even thinner up there the second time around; she wondered if her lungs would cave in from the pressure. The diving board, however, felt exactly the same as before: wobbly, slippery and terrifying. She tried not to look down.

"You can do it, Jai!" screamed Billy from far below. "Remember your dream!"

Her dream. Billy was right. In that moment, she thought about her conversation with her mother, the star and its beautiful song, and all she had learned that night. Jai *knew* those things were true. At that moment, and to her astonishment, she realized that all fear had fled her body. She stood on the perilous board, engulfed in a mysterious calm, as if a door had been slammed shut from a noisy room deep in her mind. Jai didn't understand it and she didn't know how long it would last. Without hesitation, she took a deep breath and leapt off the board.

For a split second, her body floated—suspended in the open sky. The sensation surprised her—timeless, weightless. It was the closest she had ever felt to flying. And just as quickly, she torpedoed into the water below, feet first. While it wasn't a dive exactly, it *was* a solid jump. Best of all, she didn't feel afraid anymore.

She could hear the roaring of the crowd before she emerged and broke the surface of the water like a triumphant ocean fish. Billy was the first one to congratulate her. He ran to the edge of the pool motioning for her to come quickly.

"You wouldn't believe what I just saw!" he said. "You were up there on the board and right before you jumped, I saw this—this—thing!"

"What thing?!"

"I'm not sure. It just appeared—sort of like a blast of light—and then it was gone. Whatever it was, it was pretty amazing."

"Let's ask the Water Trees about it tomorrow."

"I'm at soccer all day. Lemme know what they say."

"Deal."

They did their secret handshake, and Jai hoisted herself out of the pool.

The following afternoon, Jai raced to The Grove to announce the news about her successful jump. All of the Water Trees were elated.

Jai asked, "You know when I was up on the high dive, Billy said he saw this strange blast of light. What was that?"

The Water Trees smiled, glancing silently at one another, and said, "We are pleased that he can see such things."

Not satisfied, Jai pressed for more of an answer. The Eldest Tree would only say, "It will all become clear when it's supposed to."

There wasn't anything else to do but get back to the business at hand. She reached for the Leaf and resumed tugging away. After a while, a voice interrupted her. It was The Stem again.

"Try harder, Jai!"

She gave a solid yank. In that instant, a new and strange thing occurred. Jai could hear the faint sound of a beating drum, which seemed to spring directly from inside the Leaf itself. She could feel the rhythm pulse softly against her palms. And in a flash, it was gone.

"You have to *really* mean it!" repeated the Stem.

"What *was* THAT?!"

"Don't stop, Jai!"

Jai pulled even harder and the drumbeat returned, only this time much louder.

"You have to REALLY mean it!"

Her heart pounded furiously as she yanked and pulled. Meanwhile, the beat from inside the Leaf had grown so strong that it pulsed all the way through her fingers.

"I *DO* mean it!"

Jai tugged with all of her power as the beat of the drum grew louder and louder, faster and faster. And then, without warning, it stopped.

Clutching the Leaf, Jai felt oddly suspended in the silence.

"Well then," replied the Stem simply, "As you wish."

It broke with a gentle snap.

Flabbergasted, Jai looked at the Leaf that was now in her hands. She'd done it!

All of the Water Trees leaned towards her, wanting to see.

CHAPTER 2

"*Now* you are ready," announced the Eldest Tree. "When you mean something *that* much, you can do anything."

Jai stared at the Leaf, dumbstruck. It sparkled quietly as if to say hello.

"Go ahead, Jai. Take a look at the map."

"Where is it?"

"Turn the Leaf over," instructed the Stem.

Jai took a close look at the Stem and was surprised to see that it was wearing a miniscule pair of glasses. She hadn't noticed that before. The Stem protruded from the branch, now Leafless, looking scholarly in an odd sort of way.

"All Water Tree Leaves are designed in the same way," continued the Stem. "Blue Leaf on one side, secret map on the other."

"Oh."

Jai turned over the Leaf and stared at it, bewildered. The map was completely blank—except for a small blue dot at the western-most edge. Inspecting the dot more closely she soon recognized that it was, in fact, a perfect replica of The Water Tree Grove. But there were no other details on the map except for that one—just a vast empty space.

"Our maps are unique," noted the Eldest Tree.

Jai looked at the Tree, trying to hide her disappointment. Clearly, without any directions, the map was useless.

"Nothing of the sort!" retorted the Stem, hearing her thought. "You just don't know how to read it yet."

"Read it? But there's nothing to read!"

The Eldest Tree smiled.

"Everything is clearly laid out for you, Jai. You're currently stepping into the unknown. So—the unknown is precisely charted out for you here."

Jai scrunched her nose.

"But it doesn't show me anything!"

"You don't see anything *yet*," replied the Eldest Tree, "For that is the nature of the unknown."

"But I don't know where I'm going—and it's not showing me a route even if I did!"

"It shows you where to start from—that is enough for now."

Jai thought a moment. It was true; the map wasn't *completely* blank, it *did* indicate the Grove.

"So I start from right here?" asked Jai.

"Precisely," smiled the Eldest Tree.

Just then, the Leaf slipped from her hands, morphed into a red-tailed hawk and launched into the sky.

"Hey, come back!" shouted Jai.

The Eldest Tree chuckled heartily.

"That Leaf has a spirit as free as your own Jai. It will return, all in good time.

"But why did it have to go NOW? It just got here!"

The Water Trees glanced at each other knowingly, as if in private conversation.

"We think it's time for you to start learning the rules, Jai," announced the Eldest Tree. All of the other Water Trees nodded in agreement.

"Rules?"

Reaching up to its highest branch, the Eldest Tree retrieved an enormous golden book. The front cover, in bright blue letters, boasted the title, *"Fantastic Adventures; Not Just a Theory—Top Secret Tips of The Water Trees."*

"You guys wrote a book?"

"Go ahead, open it!"

Jai turned to the first page and read out loud: "Step One: After plucking your Leaf, you must continue to be patient."

"Indeed," replied the Trees in unison.

"Patience? THAT? Ugh!"

"You must be ready and able to read the signs, Jai."

"What signs?"

"We'll discuss that tomorrow," smiled the Tree. "In the meantime, here comes your map!"

Peering into the sky, her face went pale. A hawk was rocketing directly towards her. It swooped past her head with split-second precision, landed at her feet with a mischievous wink, and fell, like a sheet of paper, into its original shape.

Jai frowned at the Leaf.

"You almost took my head off!"

No answer.

With some hesitation, she picked it up. The Eldest Tree smiled.

"I believe you've met your match, Jai! Now, it's time for you to go. Your father will be home soon."

Off in the distance, the roar of her dad's rickety old car blasted through the neighborhood. The muffler needed replacing—it belched out a loud *VAROOOOOM!* whenever he hit the gas pedal. He'd promised to get it fixed with the next paycheck.

"One more thing before you leave," said the Eldest Tree. "It's important that you know how to carry your Leaf. While traveling, always roll it up like a cylinder and keep it tucked in your back pocket."

"That won't hurt it?"

"Nothing can possibly hurt it, Jai. This is your Leaf for life. Now, run along. We'll continue tomorrow."

Jai carefully rolled the Leaf into a scroll and gently tucked it into the back pocket of her jeans. The Stem nodded approvingly, its tiny bifocals shining in the setting sun.

"Thanks for everything, you guys. I'll see you tomorrow."

Excited and confused, Jai hugged the Eldest Tree and headed for home. As she walked, the Leaf, unnoticed, slipped from her back pocket, morphed into an enormous bald eagle and launched into the sky.

CHAPTER 3

"WHERE ARE YOU?!" Jai shouted.

"I'm right here, Honey," answered her dad from the kitchen. The oven door squeaked open as he checked on the cookies he was baking. "What's wrong?"

Not meaning to alert her father, she played along.

"Just looking for something, Dad."

"Dinner will be ready in a minute. Soup tonight!"

"Okay. Thaaaanks."

Alone in her room, panicked, she checked her back pocket, looked under the bed, searched the closet, looked out the window, and checked her back pocket again. The Leaf was gone. She must have dropped it. In a flash, she raced past the kitchen towards the front door.

"Forgot something, Dad! Be right back!"

It was beginning to get dark; she didn't have much time. Jai sped back to the Grove and retraced her steps. The Leaf was nowhere to be found. Returning to the house, she slogged into the kitchen, as her dad was serving up dinner.

Jai collapsed into a kitchen chair. "I'm not hungry."

She meant it. She felt queasy. Her entire world had just been turned inside out, and her appetite along with it.

"What's wrong, Honey?"

Her father's forehead wrinkled a little, as it always did when he was really concerned about something. Seeing this, Jai's heart sank another notch. She hated to cause him more worry.

"Do you have a fever?"

He put his hand on her forehead, checking.

"You don't feel hot."

She yearned to tell her dad about what was really happening. Like many of the adults she knew, he didn't believe in dreams and had forgotten about the magic of Water Trees. She decided to stay quiet.

"I just think I need to lie down."

"Okay, Honey. I'll check on you in a little while."

Jai left the kitchen, changed clothes, collapsed on her bed, and started to cry. Her tears rolled endlessly. Her nose ran all over the place. She had gone through almost an entire box of tissues and was blowing her nose for the millionth time when a loud tapping noise interrupted her. It came from her bedroom window.

Squinting towards the glass, she jumped. An enormous eagle had landed on the outside ledge and was pecking eagerly at the windowsill. The sight of the huge bird trying to get in through the window frightened her at first.

Distracted briefly from her misery, Jai exclaimed, "Hey, don't break my window!"

The majestic eagle looked up and immediately morphed into the Leaf.

"My Leaf!"

Jai pushed open the window, snatched it quickly from the ledge and gave it a big, long hug.

"You came back!" she shrieked.

The Leaf seemed to tolerate Jai's affection, but its brilliant blue color brightened even more.

"You can't turn into a bird in here. My dad would get REALLY upset!" Jai said, heaving a huge sigh of relief.

The Leaf nodded obediently.

"C'mon, Jai. It's getting late and it's a school day tomorrow," her dad yelled. "Come and eat something."

That's right! She thought, *tomorrow's the first day of school.* She quickly tucked the Leaf under her pillow.

"Just...stay there. Don't fly around right now! I'll be back!"

She entered the kitchen as her father was ladling out two bowls of homemade soup. Seeing her, his eyes brightened.

"You look better!"

Jai inspected his face closely, grateful that the wrinkles in his forehead had receded.

"So do you, Dad!"

The two sat across from one another at the small kitchen table. Jai loved these moments. Her dad joked with her as they competed to see who could slurp their steaming hot soup the loudest. It was the end of summer, but a brand-new beginning as far as Jai was concerned. Tomorrow, she'd tell her friends at school.

CHAPTER 4

Class had started hours ago and Jai couldn't contain it any longer. She had planned to wait until recess, but that was too far off. Billy *always* sat directly behind Jai in class and this year was no exception. Jai took a quick glance at their teacher, Ms. Hanks, who was writing an assignment on the board. Trying not to be obvious, Jai leaned back, casually turned her head and whispered to Billy.

"It happened!"

Wide-eyed, he threw up his arms in spontaneous triumph, as if he'd just scored a goal in soccer and exclaimed, "YES!!!!"

Ms. Hanks jumped sharply and her chalk made an agonizingly loud screech across the board, causing the entire class to recoil.

Ms. Hanks was pretty, but fierce. Her hair was always perfect—meticulously pulled back into a flawless, shiny bun, every strand obediently in place. What DID move around, however, were her eyebrows. She could raise them at will, one at time, emphasizing her disapproval, her amusement, or both. It was a rare skill that Jai admired and had tried to learn, time and again, without success. Despite being a "newer" teacher, Ms. Hanks acted as if she'd been there for ages. Such was her confidence.

Ms. Hanks' right eyebrow immediately shot up as she spun and instinctively located the source of disturbance.

"Perhaps you two would like to share your good news with the rest of the class? What's so exciting, Jai?"

"Oh, nothing."

"She got the Leaf!" whispered a girl who had been listening from the back row.

As if on cue, the recess bell rang. Everyone poured out into the playground and gathered around Jai.

"Where is it?" asked Billy.

"At home under my pillow. I didn't want to bring it to school because it keeps turning into a bird."

"A bird?"

"Birds are filthy," whined Natalie Snoot.

That comment didn't surprise Jai—at all. Natalie cared more about her nail polish than anything else. Jai rolled her eyes and continued.

"And there's even a book that comes with it!"

"You mean, you have to do homework?" asked one of the boys, pretending he was going to throw up.

"It's not *that* kind of book. It's really cool."

"It's not nearly as cool as my new video game," boasted Dax Googan, who was an even worse bully at school than at the town pool.

"You're just jealous," replied Billy, not feeling threatened in the least.

"No, I'm not!"

"Yes, you ARE!" retorted Jai, who wasn't afraid of Dax

either.

"Does it talk?" asked Jeffrey Hammersfield, who had hidden a crush on Jai for the past two and a half years.

"No, but it flies."

"COOL!"

"But how can it do that?" pondered Michael Peabody III. As the class brain, he wondered what biological process could result in such a thing.

"So when can we see it?" asked Patrice Zonaire, whose crushes changed weekly.

Just then the bell rang and recess was over. Billy leaned towards Jai and whispered, "Snack at your house?"

"Yeah. And the Grove after that!"

"Did your dad make cookies last night?" Billy was hopeful.

"Chocolate chip."

"SCORE!"

Jai and Billy raced for her house after school. It was a neck-and-neck tie when they got to the door. Panting hard, Jai took out her key and paused. Normally, they'd make a rush for the kitchen. This time, however, she paused and stared at the doorknob, thinking.

"C'mon, Jai. Let's go in!"

"It might be a mess in there. The Leaf turned into a bald eagle last night and almost shattered my window."

"Cool!"

"Not cool, Billy! If the place is wrecked, I have to clean it up. My dad can't know about this!"

Billy nodded.

"Don't worry. I'll help clean up if it's a disaster in there."

That was an absolute first. Never before in history had Billy *ever* volunteered to clean anything. But this was about a Water Tree Leaf, so he was willing to make an exception.

Jai turned the key and slowly opened the door, grateful to find that the house was completely quiet, everything in place. The two bounded into her room. Jai quickly fetched the Leaf from under the pillow and held it before Billy.

"Whoa!"

The Leaf shimmered in reply, morphed into a blue jay, chirped loudly, and took to the air, flapping circles around their heads.

"You can't do that in here!" shouted Jai to the bird.

The blue jay fluttered to her and instantly dropped into her hands as a Leaf.

Billy stared in amazement.

"Told ya," Jai said. "C'mon. Let's eat."

She placed the Leaf on the kitchen table, and the two friends eyed it carefully while silently devouring cookies. Billy wondered if it could turn into some sort of mini fire-spitting dragon. Jai wondered about the magical places the map led to. The Leaf simply remained a Water Tree Leaf. After their snack, she tucked the Leaf into her *front* pocket and the two friends raced to the Grove.

The Eldest Tree had been waiting for them. Jai held the Leaf, map-side-up for the Tree.

"Can't it at least show me where I'm going?"

"Well, let's see now," said the Eldest Tree. "Hmmm. Here's where we are."

With the tip of its blue branch, the Tree pointed to the left edge of the map at the miniature replica of The Water Tree Grove. Jai marveled again at how perfect it was; even the Trees' blue bark could be seen rippling in the breeze. A tiny golden arch immediately appeared next to the image of the Grove.

"This is The Arch of Light," noted the Tree. "This is where your journey begins."

Jai and Billy quietly gasped.

"Now, here's where you're going, Jai."

The Tree pointed to the opposite utmost edge—on the right side of the map—where another tiny arch simultaneously appeared. A thin line indicated a river next to it, and just beyond that sat a peculiar pinhead of light. Everything in-between remained completely blank. Jai stared closely at the speck—it looked like some sort of drum.

"A drum? I'm going to a drum?"

"You are going to *The Land of The Drum*," announced the Eldest Tree with a royal tone of finality.

And with that, the Leaf excitedly morphed into a bright red canary, flew a jubilant spiral into the air and landed on one of the higher branches of the Tree. Billy was wonderstruck.

"How does it *do* that?"

"Water Tree Leaves are free beings," explained the Tree. "All things that are free, do things spontaneously, without explanation and without warning. And, being free, they bring beauty wherever they go."

The canary immediately changed back into a Leaf and floated to the ground; its rich blue coat sparkled with gentle hues of lemon-yellow and rose. Jai knelt and carefully picked it up.

Maybe I'll pluck a Water Tree Leaf one day, mused Billy to himself. He imagined a Leaf that could change into a variety of racecars.

"Ah, you might pluck one for yourself in the future," smiled the Eldest Tree, reading his thought. "But now it's Jai's turn and your assistance will be needed here while she's on her journey."

The two friends looked at each other, perplexed.

"You'll see," continued the Tree. "Remember, Jai, this is *your* map. It is meant for you. It will always do everything it can to help you."

Upon hearing those words, the Leaf bent and nodded, as if to gently bow at her service.

"So when can I get started?"

"Tomorrow."

"Wow!"

"However, there is something very important that you *must* do first."

The Eldest Tree paused. Jai waited, wide-eyed.

"What is it?"

The Tree gazed at Jai in a way she didn't understand.

"You must say goodbye."

Now it was Jai's turn to pause. A sudden heaviness seized her heart. It never occurred to her that she'd have to say goodbye. She'd never done that before.

"Goodbye?" she asked.

"Yes, Goodbye."

"Are you sure? I thought adventures were supposed to be fun."

"It will be, Jai. But first you must say goodbye—to all of us."

On second thought, maybe I don't want a Leaf after all, thought Billy.

The Eldest Tree smiled at Billy and said nothing.

"Even Billy? Do I have to say goodbye to him?"

The Tree smiled lovingly at Jai.

"Even Billy. It's in the *Rule Book*, on page two."

Jai glanced at the *Rule Book.* It was leaning against the Tree, exactly where she had left it the day before. This time, however, the title—*Fantastic Adventures: Not Just a Theory—Top Secret Tips of the Water Trees*—gleamed brilliant gold, as opposed to the bright blue letters from the other day.

"Do the letters always change colors like that?"

"Only when there's something important for you to learn," answered the Tree.

Billy marveled at the mysterious volume. *His* schoolbooks never changed colors like that.

Jai reluctantly opened the book and turned to the second page.

"Step Two: You have to say goodbye."

For the first time in her life, she wondered if going on a Great Adventure was such a *great* idea after all. Upon hearing her thought, the Stem, who had been quietly observing the conversation, exclaimed,

"I thought you *meant* it!"

"I *did* mean it!" Jai replied.

"Turn to the next page," whispered the Eldest Tree.

Jai flipped the page and read: "Step Three: Always listen to Stems."

Jai looked up from the book. The Stem was nodding its tiny

head in proud agreement. She'd never thought about Stems being all that important in the total scheme of things.

"My Dear!" countered the Stem, hearing her thought. "We Stems have knowledge that will *astound* you!"

Jai closed the *Rule Book*—she didn't want to read anymore. The cover had changed again—this time the front letters gleamed bright orange.

"That means you REALLY need to learn this!" noted the Stem. "C'mon, Jai. Keep reading!"

Instead of opening the book, Jai looked out at the Water Trees in the Grove. She'd been with them for as long as she could remember.

"But, how can I say goodbye to all of you? That's impossible. I think saying hello makes much more sense. How about if we all say hello and then I leave?"

"No, Jai," replied the Eldest Tree. "You must say goodbye. It's a very brave thing to do."

Then her blood froze.

"What about my dad? Do I have to say goodbye to him too?"

Her lower lip began to quiver. She thought of him all alone in their small house. She'd never considered any of this before. Soon, rivers of tears rolled heavily down her cheeks. She wiped them off with the Leaf, hoping the map wouldn't smear.

"How can I leave him?"

Billy stood quiet as a stone. He refused to cry in that moment, but he wanted to.

The Eldest Tree looked down at Jai with ancient eyes.

"We'll all be there for your father, Jai."

"But he doesn't believe in you."

"Jai, there's much more to this than you currently know. Your father has a journey of his own to experience. Your mother will help with that too."

"My Mom? But he doesn't believe in that either."

"Jai, you have to trust this. Your father will be fine. Better than that. And you will see all of us again. But you have to say goodbye. This doesn't make sense to you now, but it will later."

Jai looked down at the Leaf in her hands.

"The map is for *you*, Jai. You've worked so hard to get it. It is time. Try not to worry. Just as your mother told you in your dream, we will all be watching over you."

"What do you mean?" sniffed Jai. Her nose was now officially running all over the place.

The Tree smiled sweetly.

"You'll see. Why don't you bring your friends here after school tomorrow? We'll all see you off."

It was getting late. Jai tucked the Leaf in her front pocket and gave the Tree a very, long, sad hug.

"Now, now, Jai, try not to worry. Get a good night's rest," said the Eldest Tree.

"C'mon, Jai" echoed Billy. "I'll walk with you to your house."

The Water Trees waved as Jai and Billy departed. The two friends didn't race. They didn't sprint. The weight of her pending departure slowed them both down to a mere walk.

CHAPTER 5

"Jai, you haven't said a word all night."

She and her father were sitting at the kitchen table, finishing dessert. The refrigerator whirred as she sat in silence.

"Is everything ok? Did something happen at school today?"

"No," replied Jai, repeatedly scraping the plate with her fork.

"What is it, Jai?"

She wanted to tell him everything. Not just goodbye—but *everything*: the dream, the way the star sang, the things her mom had told her, how after years of trying, she had finally succeeded in plucking the Water Tree Leaf, that she'd seen the map, and now she had to say goodbye. How could she assure him they'd see each other again because Water Trees said so, and they're always right?

Jumping from *The Nose Bleed Section* at the pool felt easy compared to blurting all of this out, but she had to try. She took a deep breath and let her words take a leap.

"Dad, a long time ago I had this dream about Mom, and she told me…"

"Jai, we've been through this, Honey. I love your mom too. I know you miss her, and I do too. But those were just dreams."

"But Dad…"

"That's enough, Jai. You're getting older now. You really have to stop this."

"Stop what?"

"Stop pretending those things are real."

Jai didn't know which hurt more—her frustration or seeing the sadness in her father's eyes.

The air in the kitchen was now clogged with silence. Neither of them spoke further. All the words she wanted to say were tangled up in a ball, lodged in her throat. Her father's lanky body drooped even further as he reached for the newspaper and snapped it open to the weather section. The wrinkles on his forehead re-surfaced as he turned the pages. Jai wondered if there was a chapter in the *Rule Book* about how to talk to adults before going on a Great Adventure. She regretted having closed it when she did. Maybe the answer was on the next page.

Both of them jumped slightly when the doorbell rang. After her dad opened the door, Jai looked up from the table, shocked. It was Natalie Snoot.

This is an absolute first, thought Jai.

Natalie had never come to visit before. She waltzed into the kitchen showing off her latest designer clothing. Her nails sparkled; her red hair bounced with dazzling shine. Even if Jai and her dad *did* have that kind of money, Jai would never want to dress that way. Natalie was a mannequin straight out of the box.

Her father pulled up a third chair and was the first one to speak.

"Natalie, would you like some dessert?"

"No thanks, it'll ruin my complexion," Natalie replied dryly, primping her ultra-conditioned hair.

Her dad grinned.

"Honey, you're only ten years old."

Jai rolled her eyes. The night had gone from bad to worse. But then she had an idea.

"Um...Dad? Can Natalie and I go to my room to study for a while?"

"Well, yes, for a little while."

"C'mon, Natalie, let's go."

And with that, the two girls went off to her room. Jai took a quick last peek out the door and quickly closed it behind them.

"What are you doing here?" asked Jai. She always got straight to the point.

"I heard you're leaving tomorrow. Is that true?"

"Yeah. I'm feeling pretty scared about it, but it's time. I'm still trying to tell my dad."

"Yeah, that's a hard one. More like impossible. What did the Water Trees say?"

"Basically not to worry about it. That everything will be ok."

"Well, then that's your answer. You know they're always right."

Jai smiled. Even though Natalie was hopelessly obsessed with her nails, she still was a kid who believed in Water Trees. All the kids did. It helped to talk with someone, anyone, who understood.

"Well, I just wanted to give you something," continued Natalie. "It's a gift."

Natalie reached into her Geechee designer purse and retrieved a small golden cylinder.

"Here. This is for you."

"What is it?"

"Lipstick."

"Lipstick?"

Natalie's face lit up as she took the lid off the cylinder for Jai to see.

"Not only lipstick! This is part of the new Perma-Lip series for Women-On-the-Go. They say it'll adhere to the lip membrane for over 96 hours—perfect for travel!"

"Natalie, that's *disgusting.*" Jai was thoroughly uninterested, yet, nonetheless, genuinely moved by the gesture. "Maybe I can use it as a permanent marker."

The two girls looked at one another, not knowing what else to say. Throughout most of their childhood, they argued over just about everything.

"Whatever," shrugged Natalie, and then with a smile added, "I'll miss you anyway."

"Me too. Thanks for the gift."

The two girls gave each other an awkward hug.

Water Trees had that sort of effect on people—once you love a Water Tree, you just naturally start appreciating people even if they annoy you. Such was the case for Jai and Natalie. As for the Water Trees, they simply love everyone—whoever they are—even adults who don't believe in them.

Jai saw Natalie to the door.

"Meet us at The Water Tree Grove after school tomorrow," whispered Jai.

"The whole class already knows about it. We'll all be there."

"And thanks for the marker."

"It's *lipstick*, Jai."

"Yeh, lipstick, whatever—thanks though."

Jai closed the door and walked into her dad's bedroom. He was already fast asleep.

She decided she'd say goodbye after school before going to the Grove—he'd be home between shifts. She still didn't know how she'd do it, but her heart felt lighter. As she softly kissed him goodnight, she noticed that the wrinkles had once again receded from his forehead. Relieved, she returned to her room to pack.

So far, her packing list currently included the two items resting on her bed: her Leaf and her favorite rock. Jai always liked to travel light and figured that Great Adventures should be no exception. After all, what's so great about having to lug around a ton of stuff? Inspecting her room, she realized that she'd almost forgotten the photo on her dresser. The snapshot was of Jai and her parents. Taken a few months after she was born, it showed her young mother and father beaming proudly at the tiny bundle in their arms. It was hard for Jai to imagine ever being that small. Her dad said that it had been taken before the war. The photo had a wooden frame and Jai always placed it so she could easily see it from her bed.

Jai didn't really know what it meant to be in a war, or why there were ever any wars in the first place. She only knew that her mom had been killed in one. Whenever she asked her father about it, he would always say the same thing.

"She just happened to be in the wrong place at the wrong time, Honey."

"What do you mean?"

But that question was always met with silence. Her dad would give her a sad smile, a gentle kiss and usually reach for the newspaper.

Jai took the picture out of the frame and placed it on her bed with the other items. One, two, three. Her packing list was complete.

Satisfied, she picked up her favorite rock. It was only about the size of a quarter but if you looked closely, you could see a mini-galaxy. The stone was filled with speckled colors that danced gloriously when held in the sun. She'd had it for years, ever since her very first camping trip with her dad. Jai rubbed its smooth surface between her thumb and forefinger and then angled it to catch the light of her reading lamp. She admired its amazing pattern of swirls and then dropped it into her pocket. *"Done."* She put the photo in the left back pocket of her jeans. *"Check."*

The Leaf, in the meantime, had been sitting on the bed. It immediately transformed into a raven, hopped onto her dresser and cawed softly while trying to open the top drawer with its beak.

"Shhhhhhhhh! My dad's asleep!"

The raven sharply cocked its jet-black head at Jai and then back towards the window.

"Okay, I guess you want out."

Jai opened her window and, in a flash, the bird swooped into the nighttime sky.

"Just don't peck on the glass when you come back!" Jai whispered loudly after him. "I'll keep the window open."

The raven cawed in return as it flew, its shining black feathers soaked in moonlight. Jai decided to finish packing in the morning—especially since a third of her provisions had just flown off without her.

Once in bed, she gazed out her window and searched for The Great Arch of Light. After scanning the horizon several times, she lazily drifted off to sleep. Deep in the night, without a sound, the Leaf returned through the window and rested next to her pillow.

CHAPTER 6

"What's *wrong* with you people?!" exclaimed Ms. Hanks to the class, fierce as ever. "Did *anyone* do their homework last night?"

In fact, everyone *had* done their homework, but it didn't seem to matter.

The entire class was distracted, restless, and answering the simplest questions incorrectly. Even Robert Peabody Smith III, the Class Brain, couldn't seem to get anything right. Today was the BIG FAREWELL. It was impossible to concentrate. Everyone kept passing notes to Jai, who was trying her best to hide them inconspicuously under her books. It wasn't working.

Ms. Hanks spied the growing mound of paper on Jai's desk.

"What's going on, Jai?"

Jai's mouth ran dry.

"Uh, nothing, Ms. Hanks."

"Everyone seems to be very interested in you today," Ms. Hanks said, raising her brow.

"Really?" Jai's voice cracked.

"I suggest you ALL get yourselves under control, or the ENTIRE CLASS will have to stay after school!"

A sudden hush enveloped the room. It was so quiet you could hear an ant crawl.

Billy leaned forward and shot a wide-eyed glance at Jai as if to say, *NO WAY!* She glared back and under her breath said, "Don't blow it, Billy. Just this once, BEHAVE!"

Billy nodded back as if to say, *Okay.*

From then on, the class did its best to stay focused on their work. It felt like an eternity. Actually, to Jai, it felt like several eternities in a row.

"Today we're going to talk about circles," announced Ms. Hanks. "Everything—EVERYTHING moves in circles and patterns—from atoms, to oceans, from planets to entire galaxies!"

She opened her right desk drawer (the left drawer was always mysteriously locked), and retrieved a small collection of shells.

"Notice how the swirling pattern in the snail shell looks just like the swirling pattern in this seashell. All of nature moves in circles!"

The only circle Jai was interested in was the clock that ticked from above the chalkboard. And she wished that the orbit of the minute hand *would speed it up* already.

"This is far more interesting than you think, Jai!" Ms. Hanks had read her thoughts. She was good at that sort of thing. "I suggest you pay close attention!"

For the rest of the morning and throughout the afternoon, Jai tried her best, until at last the final bell rang.

Her classmates piled out of class, but Jai stayed behind. She had a job to do. Once alone, she slowly approached Ms. Hanks, who was already engrossed in grading papers at her desk. Jai awkwardly cleared her throat.

"Uh, Ms. Hanks?"

"Why, yes, Jai." She replied, surprised to see Jai anywhere near school after the final bell.

"I just wanted to say thanks."

"Thanks?" Ms. Hanks' eyebrow shot up in curiosity.

"Well, yes. Thanks."

"Are you feeling alright, Jai?"

"Yeah."

"Well, you're welcome," smiled Ms. Hanks. "What are you thanking me for, Jai?"

"I've learned a lot in your class. I just want you to know that I really appreciate it."

Jai shot a quick glance out the window and noticed her eavesdropping friends unsuccessfully hidden just below the class window. She pulled her shoulders back and tried to smooth her composure.

"What's going on, Jai?"

Ms. Hanks' eyes were now locked on her. Jai looked down at her hands, speechless. She knew she had to say goodbye, but she just didn't know how to say it.

"I guess I'd better go now."

Jai took a deep breath and quickly blurted, "Goodbye!" as she turned around and raced for the door. Ms. Hanks' right eyebrow shot up to her hairline as she watched Jai attempt her escape. Grinning, she put down her red pencil.

"Hmmm. Well, I'll be. You've been reading that *Rule Book*, haven't you?"

"What?" asked Jai, spinning back around.

"*The Rule Book*," repeated Ms. Hanks. "You've been reading it!"

"You KNOW about that?"

Jai was flabbergasted.

"Why ELSE would anyone waltz up here to say 'goodbye' like that? Really, Jai, you should have come more prepared. That was a...less than stellar 'goodbye.'"

"I—Uh... "

"When a person says goodbye before going on a Great Adventure," continued Ms. Hanks, her voice carrying the definitive authority of a teacher, "it should be done with the utmost respect, gratitude and appreciation of the person you're saying goodbye to. It's not a task to discharge as quickly as possible, like taking out the trash! Really, Jai!"

"Uh... "

"*You* think that just because I'm an adult, I don't know about Water Trees!" Ms. Hanks was now grinning broadly.

Jai could only stand there in shock, her mouth opened so wide that her tonsils screamed for privacy. The rest of the class remained clumped together outside the window, frozen in disbelief.

"Not *all* adults have forgotten about Water Trees, Jai. *Most*, but not all."

And with that, she resumed grading her papers.

"Uh... "

"Go on, now," instructed Ms. Hanks, motioning towards Jai with her red pencil.

"Well, goodbye, Ms. Hanks," declared Jai. "And thank you." It felt much easier to say it sincerely the second time.

"Better," noted Ms. Hanks, "but it still needs some work. I'd give it a 'B.' Put more heart into it the next time."

Never in a million years would Jai have thought she'd actually be graded on how to say a sincere *goodbye* before going off on a Great Adventure. There wasn't anything else to say after that, not that Jai could manage any more words at that moment anyway. Ms. Hanks had already returned to her work. And so, Jai simply turned around and walked out the door—stunned.

Once outside the building, she was swamped by her equally dumbfounded classmates.

"How could a teacher know about Water Trees?!" exclaimed Billy, looking like he'd seen a ghost.

"I have no idea," mumbled Jai, still in shock.

"Let's go ask the Trees," suggested Natalie Snoot, who had just applied a heaping layer of Perma-Lip to her narrow mouth. Her lips gleamed in a startling, radioactive sort of way. Billy squinted at the glare.

"What happened to your mouth?"

"You're too unrefined to understand," yawned Natalie, holding her hand out to inspect her nails.

"Look, you guys," interrupted Jai. "I have to go say goodbye to my dad. I'll meet you over there."

Her dad was sitting in the kitchen, reading the newspaper, relaxing before his next shift. He had carefully placed a large plate of cookies at the center of their small table. Jai wasn't hungry; her concerns about how to say goodbye had stolen her appetite. Regardless, she popped a cookie in her mouth, figuring that chewing would give her time to find the right words. Her father found some first.

"Jai, about last night—I love you, Honey. But you really need to stop talking about these...dreams of yours. We've already discussed this. I know it's hard, Honey, it's hard for me too. But your mom will not be coming back."

Jai chewed and took a quick gulp.

"But Dad, those dreams are real."

His face stiffened and he drew a heavy sigh. There wasn't any way to convince him and she knew she was running out of time.

"Jai, you're just as stubborn as your mother!"

She smiled at this, immensely pleased with the idea.

"Dad, just promise me one thing. If Mom comes to you in a dream, just try to believe it. OK?"

Her father once again decided to play along. "All right, Jai. I promise."

She knew he didn't really mean it, but that would have to be good enough for now. Now that she was in this deep, she figured she might as well go for it all.

"And promise that you'll go to the Water Trees sometime and listen to them. Make sure to bring a pen and paper and take good notes."

Her father looked at her with concern. He knew that she loved to play at The Water Tree Grove. For years, it had provided some sort of a secret club for all the kids in town. But that's all it was—a children's game.

"Jai, you're ten years old now, Honey. You really need to grow out of this."

"Dad, please promise!"

Her father took a deep breath and stared at his daughter.

"Honey, I have to leave for work soon. Let's talk about something else."

"Dad, you have to promise!"

Her father paused, held up his right hand as if taking an oath, and proclaimed, "OK, I promise!"

There was an edge of mockery in his voice. Jai didn't care. That would have to do.

Without saying another word, she got up from her chair and hugged him with all her strength. She felt her love and gratitude for him swell in her chest as she softly kissed him goodbye.

"What's *that* for?"

"Oh, nothing."

"I love you, Pumpkin. I wish I didn't have to leave for work right now, but I do."

She gave him another hug and buried her face in his shirt. How could she leave him? Her heart felt like a busted egg—a raw and oozing mess. While her face was still pressed hard into her father's chest, an unmistakable image appeared deep in her mind—sort of like a dream, but she was awake. The Water Trees were smiling peacefully, waving to her. And there, on the lowest branch of the Eldest Tree, sat a _very_ annoyed Stem holding a miniscule sign that read: "You said you MEANT it!"

Jai gulped. The Stem was right. It was time to go. Taking a deep breath, Jai released her grip and looked directly into her father's soft brown eyes.

"I love you, Dad. You're the most amazing person I know." With another quick kiss to his cheek, she smiled and said, "Bye. See you later."

And with that, they were both out the door. Her father was getting into their old clunky car, when he suddenly stopped.

"What's *that*? What a beautiful color! Where'd you get that, Jai?"

Her Water Tree Leaf was protruding slightly from the front pocket of her jeans. Jai was dumbfounded. He noticed! But before she could reply, he was already in the car and backing out the driveway.

He shouted out the window, 'Tell me later, I'm gonna to be late for work. Bye, Honey!"

"Goodbye, Dad," whispered Jai as she waved from the driveway.

CHAPTER 7

Jai sprinted to the Grove. A breeze picked up from the east, cooling her skin and parting her short, straight hair. Along with it came a surprising sense of relief and certainty that she was doing the right thing. Her body felt lighter. Gravity had loosened its grip and, with each stride, she sped through the air in abandon—swift and free as a leaf in flight.

Jai's friends were already gathered at the Grove when she arrived. The Eldest Tree smiled, immensely pleased.

"Hello Jai! How did it go?"

"Pretty good. My dad promised to try to believe it—I mean, in case you guys ever talk to him. I don't think he really meant it, though."

The Water Trees nodded in silent understanding.

"That's a good start," replied the Eldest Tree. "As promised, we will all be watching over him. He'll understand eventually, Jai, when he's no longer in False Time."

The Water Trees often warned of False Time. None of the kids understood what that meant. Jai looked at the Tree, perplexed.

"But what IS False Time? I still don't get it."

"Be glad you don't. The only way to understand False Time

is to experience it."

"But what *exactly* does that mean? False Time?" pressed Robert Peabody Smith III, the Class Brain. Even *he* didn't get it.

"When you forget who you really are, you fall into False Time."

Jai quickly concluded that it was impossible to comprehend how anyone could forget who they are. After all, she was simply herself. The Water Trees are simply who they are. How can anyone forget something like that? She'd forgotten her books at school once, but that was about it.

"Well, what about Ms. Hanks?" asked Billy. "She must be the queen of False Time. She's always making me stay after class."

The Eldest Tree chuckled.

"Ahhhh, Ms. Hanks will be a great ally to all of you."

"But she's MEAN!" exclaimed Billy.

"She's SHARP, Billy. There's a difference."

Billy knew not to argue. After all, the Water Trees are always right, especially when you don't understand what they're saying.

"You will see," assured the Water Tree. "But only when it's time."

The Stem sat on its branch, eyeing Billy with an air of pompous disapproval.

"Hmmf! The boy's not exactly a shining monolith of intellectual achievement!"

"Now, now," replied the Water Tree, "All of this is new to him. Have patience."

Meanwhile the class looked at one another, surprised. In all their years at the Grove, they'd never even noticed a Stem, let alone heard it speak.

"Who said that?" asked Natalie Snoot, her lips glowing unnaturally in the afternoon sun.

"I did," answered the Stem with great pride. "And what on earth happened to your mouth?"

"That's enough!" interrupted the Water Tree, gentle but firm.

Jai decided to step in.

"Um, let me introduce you guys. Everybody, this is the Stem that I pulled my Leaf from. Stem, these are my friends from school."

"Greetings," offered the Stem.

"Hi," replied her friends, in unison.

"Now, Jai, let's get down to business," continued the Eldest Tree. "First of all, we see you've been keeping the Leaf in your front pocket. From now on, place it in your *back* pocket so it is always free to get out and fly whenever it needs to. All things that are free must be free to come and go, just like you. In respecting its freedom, it will always return to you. You've experienced this already."

Jai took the Leaf from her front pocket.

"But what if I sit on it?"

"Don't worry. It can take care of itself. No harm will come to it, as long as you let it be free."

"Got it!"

"Now, about getting lost..."

"Lost?" She didn't want to think about that part. Neither did her friends.

"This is a Great Adventure, Jai, so it's possible. If you ever think you've taken a wrong turn, all you need to do is roll the Leaf up like a telescope and look through it. It will show you exactly how to get back to where you were before you got off track. The Leaf will always help you get you back on course."

"That's pretty cool," commented Billy, relieved.

"Now Jai, do you understand what to do if you get lost?" asked The Eldest Tree.

"Yes."

"Good. Let's continue then. The next thing to remember is to use *all* the gifts that come to you. Some gifts don't look like gifts at the time, but they're gifts just the same. Remember to *use* them, for *that* is, and always has been, the key to having a successful Great Adventure."

Jai realized that she had forgotten to take Natalie's Perma-Lip canister out of her pants pocket from the night before. She decided to keep it with her. Maybe she'd need a permanent marker after all.

"Next are the signs," continued the Eldest Tree. "Just remember to read them."

"Got it!"

"Good! We are almost done. Now, look up. What do you see?"

Jai and her friends all craned their necks, glancing upwards.

"You mean...the sky?"

"Indeed!" answered the Eldest Tree. "This is very important. All Great Adventures include talking to it!"

Jai nodded, promising to remember.

"And one last thing!" added the Stem, adjusting its tiny bifocals.

"Ah, yes! *That*! Very important indeed!" replied the Tree, reading the Stem's thought.

"We have a question!" announced the Stem. "What do you do if you feel stuck?"

Jai frowned.

"Stuck? What do you mean?"

"What if you've done everything you've been told so far and you still find yourself in a...predicament...shall we say?" inquired the Stem.

Jai had the uneasy feeling that she was taking a pop quiz. The thought of being stuck was unsettling. She nervously fingered her front pockets.

"What kind of predicament?"

"Doesn't matter. You're going on a Great Adventure—it could happen. So...what do you do?"

Jai looked at her friends. Her friends looked back at her. Everyone shrugged.

"Uh—I—uh, don't...know?"

The Stem shook its tiny head back and forth in disappointment.

"Really, Jai! *That's* your answer?!"

"But I *don't* know!"

"Think!"

"Um...try harder?"

The Stem paused and put its tiny hand on its hip (a nob in this case).

"How about: *ask for help!*"

"Oh, yeah. OK—Got it."

"And then pay attention!" continued the Stem. "Help *will* come. Just remember: *how* it comes is optional."

"Optional?"

"Optional!" answered all the Water Trees in unison.

"What do you mean?" asked Jai, confused. Even Michael Peabody III was scratching his head over that one.

"Don't worry, Jai," answered the Eldest Tree. "The main thing to remember is that it's very important to ask for help when you need it. Don't think that you have to figure it all out alone. Help will come. The form it comes in may be...surprising."

Jai and her friends shot quick glances at one another.

"There are always helpers along the way," noted the Eldest Tree. "Some are people, some are not."

The Stem nodded proudly upon hearing this.

"You'll know which people to trust by our color blue," continued the Tree.

"Huh? Are there blue people over there?"

"Not at all. You'll understand...soon."

"...okay..."

"Good. Now, I suppose you're wondering how to get to the first Arch!"

"You mean I can start right now?"

"That's correct. After *we* say goodbye."

Silence.

The heavy hand of gravity regained its grip on Jai's entire body. Her heart sank to her feet, which now felt glued to the ground. Jai didn't know how she could possibly say goodbye to the Water Trees or to her friends—especially Billy. She didn't speak. Overwhelmed, she stood frozen.

"Jai," whispered a beautiful voice.

Everyone—except the Water Trees—looked around, wondering where the voice was coming from.

"Jai," repeated the voice, loving and pure as if soaked in starlight.

Jai stood completely still, bewildered and hopeful.

"Mom? Mom, where are you?"

"Jai, it's time to go now."

Hearing the love in her mother's words, Jai's heart melted, and she began to cry. Her mother was nowhere to be seen; yet all could hear her, as if she was everywhere at once.

"Believe in yourself, Jai," instructed her mother. "It's time now."

A soft breeze hushed through the Grove, carrying the gentle fragrance of roses. The voice was gone.

No one said a word. Not even the Stem, who was now weeping and clutching a miniature tissue in its tiny hand.

Jai took a deep breath and slowly rolled the magnificent Leaf into a scroll. After tucking it into the back pocket of her jeans, she looked out at the Water Trees with newfound determination and softly whispered:

"Goodbye."

"Goodbye, Jai," answered the Trees in unison.

One by one, Jai hugged them all. She saved the Eldest Tree for last. Reaching into her pocket, she retrieved her favorite rock and gently placed it next to the Tree's trunk.

"This is my favorite rock in the whole world. You already know that. I hope you like it." With all her heart, she hugged the Eldest Tree goodbye.

"Ms. Hanks has taught you well," smiled the Eldest Tree. "Now *this* is a proper goodbye."

Jai smiled wryly.

"She gave me a 'B.'"

Turning to her friends, Jai hugged them one by one. When she got to Billy, they did their secret handshake and promised each other to always be best friends. She couldn't imagine life without their races, their jokes, their snacks, or any of the other zillion things they always did together.

"You will see each other again," noted the Tree, reading her thought.

The two friends nodded as the Leaf slipped from her pocket. It immediately morphed into an enormous eagle and perched on her shoulder. Her friends were stunned. The Eldest Tree chuckled.

"Looks like your Leaf is ready to go!"

In that instant, it morphed back into a Leaf and fell to the ground. Jai picked it up and returned it to her back pocket.

"I guess I'm ready too."

Delighted, the Eldest Tree pointed east with its highest branch.

"Walk in this direction, Jai. You'll see the Arch in no time. Walk well. We are so very proud of you."

Jai took another deep breath as the Eldest Tree addressed her friends.

"Now, each of you has a job to do: *See* Jai safe and well. *See* that deep in your mind. This will be of great assistance to your friend."

"We can do that!" answered Billy, giving Jai a thumbs-up.

"Thanks, you guys."

"Remember to keep walking, Jai," instructed the Tree. "We will always be with you."

Jai paused and gulped down one more dry breath.

"Okay, here goes."

Jai took a first halting step. Holding back a trembling lower lip, she tried again. Her heart teetered and wobbled as she struggled to walk with confidence. Step after cautious step, she inched her way forward. Eventually she found her stride, or at least a nervous version of it. For the Water Trees, this was a day of great celebration. They would often say that courage is one of the greatest things to celebrate.

Everyone—the Water Trees, her friends, the Stem with its soggy handkerchief—cheered as they waved goodbye. Jai could hear them in the distance. She didn't know it was possible to feel so many things at once. Her heart pounded with excitement, sadness, bravery and fear, all at the same time.

"*Remember to keep walking,*" she repeated to herself.

The melody of cheers grew smaller and smaller, eventually fading out completely. All she could hear now was the rhythmic crunch of her footsteps on dry grass.

She suddenly stopped cold and looked up in astonishment. There, in the distance, stood The Great Arch of Light, sparkling under the open sky.

CHAPTER 8

BZZZZZZZZZ!

"Ouch!"

Jai had just been bitten by a Mosquito.

BZZZZZ!

"Ouch!"

Jai slapped her arm where the Mosquito had snatched another bite.

"Hey, you almost squashed me!" shouted the Mosquito.

"Well, that's what you get for biting me!"

Jai scratched her bites and grabbed the Leaf from her back pocket to inspect the map. No new images had yet appeared. And there *definitely* was no mention of talking mosquitoes.

"You won't find me in there," remarked the Mosquito, who was now reading the map over her shoulder.

"You know what this is?"

"Of course I do. I know a Water Tree Leaf when I see one."

"You know about Water Trees?"

"Of course. *They're* the ones who sent me to you."

"What?"

"I've been assigned to you."

"Huh?"

"You're going to *The Land of The Drum*, aren't you?"

"Well...yeah."

"Well, I'm here to help you get there."

"You?"

"Of course, me. It's in *The Rule Book* on page four."

"Uh, I only read the first couple of pages."

The Mosquito glared at Jai with judging eyes. "You're on a Great Adventure and you didn't read the entire *Rule Book*?"

Embarrassed, Jai tucked the Leaf back in her pocket.

"Well...yeah. But there's nothing I can do about that now, so you might as well tell me what's on the next page."

"You will be greeted by an insect," replied the Mosquito.

"What are you *talking* about?"

"That's what it says on page four. *'You will be greeted by an insect.'*"

"You didn't greet me, you *bit* me. TWICE!"

"Well, I had to get your attention somehow, Jai! It's not *my* fault that you didn't notice the first sign!"

"I didn't?"

"Nope. You just walked right on by. Really, you need to pay more attention!"

It was true. In her excitement after seeing The Great Arch of Light, Jai had forgotten everything else and eagerly marched her way right for it.

She smiled sheepishly.

"Sorry."

"Well, don't just stand there. Turn around!"

Jai had never considered obeying a mosquito before.

Regardless, she did as she was told. There, about thirty feet away stood a small wooden sign jutting out of the ground. Indeed, she had walked right past it.

"Go on, Jai. Read it!"

She walked over to it and read:

LISTEN FOR THE DRUM
SO FAR AWAY, YET NEAR.
OPEN YOUR HEART
AND YOU WILL
ALWAYS HEAR.

"Well?" asked the Mosquito, now zipping circles around Jai's head.

"Well, what?" replied Jai, shooing the Mosquito away with her hands.

"Do you hear it?"

"I can't hear anything when you're buzzing around like this!"

"Oh, sorry."

The Mosquito flew several feet away and hovered excitedly in the distance.

Jai tilted her right ear towards the sky and listened. She was astonished to hear several Drums beating faintly in the distance.

The rhythm seemed to be coming from beyond The Great Arch of Light. Jai could feel the rhythmic pulse all the way down to her toes. Enthralled, she walked slowly towards the Arch. Her heart and fingers tapped along, relishing every beat. Then, in a flash, all was silent. Jai stood completely still, dumbstruck.

"What just happened?"

"Now," announced the Mosquito in a majestic tone, "your Great Adventure has officially begun."

Jai looked at the Mosquito, eagerly anticipating further instruction.

"That's it, Jai. Nothing more for now."

"But I don't get it!"

"This is a Great Adventure. You can't expect to understand everything all at once."

And with that, it flew away.

BZZZZZZZZZZZZZZZZzzzzzzzzzzzzzzzzzzzzzzzzzzzzzzzzZzzzzzzzz zzzzzzzzz

"Hey, what's your name?"

It was too late. The Mosquito was gone, leaving Jai just footsteps away from The Great Arch of Light.

More like a royal doorway, The Great Arch stood the height of a large tree, with enough space for four people to easily pass through while walking side-by-side. It flickered with an endless bounty of bright golden flecks—tiny pinheads of light that danced and swirled, exuding a warm, peaceful glow.

As she walked towards it, her fingertips began to tingle. Once directly underneath the Arch, her entire body felt infused with a joyful strength she'd never known; like she could do *anything*, and probably *would*. In that moment, she remembered a diagram Ms. Hanks had shown during science class. It was a chart of how cells move. Jai never really thought about her cells much. But there, under The Great Arch, she could feel every single one of them dazzling in ecstatic light, twirling along with all the golden flecks that zoomed within the Arch itself.

By the time she reached the other side, she felt joyous, alive and utterly brand new. Tall green hills welcomed her from all sides, rolling along, soaked in sun. She soon noticed a sign stuck into the ground up ahead and ran to it.

NOW THAT YOUR
JOURNEY HAS LONG
LAST BEGUN, LOOK
FOR THE LEATHER,
LOOK FOR THE SUN.

Jai read it several times, trying to make sense of it. She jumped at the sound of someone shouting in the distance.

"Well, hello there!" An old man was waving to her from atop a hill in the distance. "C'mon! I've been waiting for you." He turned around and started walking down the other side of the slope, waving for her to follow. Jai raced after him.

Out of breath, she reached the valley between the two hills to find the old man sitting casually at a small table under the shade of an umbrella. A pitcher of lemonade and two empty glasses were on the table. The old man had a friendly face. His long gray hair was pulled back into a ponytail, held together by a hair tie. When he turned his head, Jai saw that it was the exact color as the Water Trees. He smiled and waved.

"Hey there! Nice to see you again!"

That's when she remembered. She'd seen him in a dream. At the time he was wearing sunglasses and eating a banana.

"Hi! Nice to see you too!"

"Thirsty? C'mon and have a glass of lemonade."

"Thanks!"

Jai took a seat. The old man poured two tall glasses of lemonade. The ice cubes clinked as they made contact with the liquid. Jai's mouth watered. Meanwhile, the Water Tree Leaf slipped from Jai's back pocket and morphed into a small green hummingbird, its wings whirring softly as it darted from glass to glass. It took tiny sips from each before coming to rest on Jai's shoulder.

"I hope you don't mind my Leaf drinking from your glass."

"Oh no, that's just fine."

Satisfied, the hummingbird darted towards the Sky, transformed into a hawk and began making slow circles high above. Jai liked the old man immediately. He had an easy, relaxed manner that reminded her of the Water Trees.

"Am I dreaming right now? I mean, I don't remember going to sleep or anything."

The old man grinned.

"Nope, you're not dreaming. You'll learn to recognize the difference. At this moment, I'd say you're very much awake! My name's Earl, by the way."

"Hi. I'm Jai."

The two shook hands. Jai was surprised by his strength, especially for an old man. Earl shot a quick glance at the hawk overhead and nodded to her.

"I see you finally plucked off that Water Tree Leaf."

"You know about Water Trees?"

"Sure do. We're old friends. I know a little something about the leaves too. Did the Stem give you a hard time?"

"More or less."

"Well, Stems can be that way. It's good to listen to them, though. Did you say goodbye?"

"Yes."

"Now, that's real good," replied Earl in a slow gentle voice. "Takes a lot of courage to do that sort of thing. Now that you've done that, you're free to say hello to everything else."

Jai smiled. She'd never thought of it that way before. "You know. How did you...?"

She was interrupted by the faint sound of beating drums. The beautiful cadence was unmistakable. It seemed to come from inside the wind itself. And just as suddenly as it appeared, it abruptly vanished.

"My, oh my. You're on a Great Adventure, all right!" beamed Earl. "The drum is a very special thing, ya know."

"I don't really know anything about it."

"Well, The drum is calling you, that's for sure. That's all you need to know for now."

Earl smiled and raised his glass.

"Here's to Great Adventures!"

"To Great Adventures!"

They clinked their glasses and took a sip. The lemonade was sweet and delicious.

"So," continued Earl, "what do you know about The Leather and The Sun?"

"Nothing. I just read about it."

"Well, I know a little bit. It's very, very old."

"'It?' It's not two things?"

"The Leather and The Sun *are* two things, but they work as one."

"As one? What do you mean?"

Earl took a long, slow sip of lemonade. He knew how to take time with things.

"Well, you're going to have to find that fire. Then you'll start to understand."

"A fire? What fire?"

"Now, Jai, it wouldn't be a Great Adventure if I told you everything!"

"Well, what do I do when I find it?"

Earl grinned.

"You'll have to find that out when you get there."

"But I don't even know where THERE is!"

Earl gazed at the hawk overhead.

"That's what Leaves are for, Jai. You best take a look."

Jai peered into the sky and gasped. The hawk was no longer circling. It was now flying away.

"You better go follow!"

Jai sprang to her feet while Earl sipped his lemonade. The hawk was now a small dot in the distance.

"I can't run that fast!"

"Just keep walking, Jai. It'll keep track of you."

"Ok. Hey, thanks for the lemonade! I hope we meet again."

"I'm sure we will," nodded Earl with a slow, easy smile. "In the meantime, don't forget to talk to the Sky."

"Thanks, Earl!"

Jai took off, sprinting up and down hill after hill, chasing an unusually carefree hawk that didn't seem to notice.

CHAPTER 9

The muscles in Jai's legs screamed. She'd been running all day. Seemingly unconcerned, the hawk continued on its way, across the late afternoon sky. Exhausted, Jai paused at the top of a hill to catch her breath. While hunched over and panting heavily, something caught her eye. A small bright light flickered from the valley below. Squinting towards it, her breath slowed with relief. It was a campfire. Jai straightened her back, stretched painfully and hobbled down the hill.

As she approached it, Jai realized this was no ordinary fire. It left no trace of smoke. Instead, the sweet fragrance of roses wafted in the air. Jai stood before the mysterious flames, thinking about her mother.

"Hello," offered a soft woman's voice. It was the Fire. The flames gently turned to rainbows as it spoke. Jai was stunned.

"Hi. Uh—may I ask, what kind of fire are you anyway?"

"I fell from the sky a long, long time ago. I wasn't always what you see now. I was a Star at one time."

"You were?"

"Indeed."

Wait'll Billy hears about this! Jai thought excitedly.

She peered into the magnificent flames. Jai had never

spoken to a member of the cosmos before—at least not at such close range. She wondered if she'd dare ask a question about the secrets of the Universe. Maybe just one secret. Start simple and take it from there...

"I will give you three," answered the Fire, hearing her thoughts. "Three secrets. If you will make a promise in return."

Jai smiled, delighted.

"Three secrets for one promise? That's sounds like a good deal! What do I need to promise?"

"To do all you can to not fall into False Time."

Jai looked curiously at the Fire. She had no interest in False Time and already knew it was something to avoid—even though she didn't really know what it was.

"There will come a time when you will meet it face-to-face," continued the Fire, "and when you do, you will have to make a choice."

Jai thought a moment and shrugged, concluding that receiving three secrets of the Universe was more than worth the trade.

"Ok. I promise!"

Pleased with her reply, the Fire sparkled with bright flecks of magenta and gold.

"Good. Secret number one: We have more in common than you think. The stars see all people, just as you see us."

Jai's eyes widened.

"You shine just as we do," continued the Fire. "We Stars are simply able to see this sort of thing more easily."

"I didn't know that!"

"Indeed. Now, for the second secret. Remember this, Jai: To grow in strength and power, you must let your mind be a mirror—not a camera."

Jai tilted her head, confused.

"What does that mean?"

"You will see," answered the Fire softly.

At that very moment, the faint beating of drums swept through the air and then vanished.

"Ah, you're going to *The Land of The Drum!*" The flames leapt into the shape of a circle, spinning colors and the scent of roses all around. "So you must be looking for The Leather and the Sun."

Jai heaved a sigh of relief. Things were finally starting to come together... hopefully.

"Do you know where it is?"

"Better than that—here is the third secret. Stand back for a moment."

The Fire crackled loudly, producing a bright spark that sent three small golden seeds bursting forth like popcorn and hurling through the air. Remarkably, the seeds stopped mid-flight, hovered for a moment and, like milkweed thistle, floated slowly to the ground.

"These are a gift from the sun. Let them cool off before picking them up."

Jai waited as the seeds glowed silently before her. Eventually, they cooled down to a hue of soft gold. Each seed was a perfect orb with a hole running through its center.

"Thanks! How are these a secret?"

"That's for you to discover, Jai."

She inspected the seeds and decided to ask a more practical question, hoping to get a practical answer.

"What are the holes for?"

"The Leather and The Sun is very powerful. But you'll have to do some work so that it will work for you."

Jai had been mistaken. Things were actually making less sense. Not only that, she was getting hungry.

Just then, an enormous hawk descended from the sky at breakneck speed, brushing Jai's cheek with the tip of its left wing before landing at her feet. It had been carrying something in its talons. Remarkably, it brought her a sandwich and then instantly transformed back into a Leaf.

"That's quite a Leaf you've got there," noted the Fire.

Jai nodded, chewing heartily. She had no idea where the sandwich had come from, but not much of anything had made sense today. She kissed the Leaf, trying not to get crumbs on it, and tucked it in the back pocket of her jeans.

"Some answers await you just beyond these hills," said the Fire. "Look for a special tree. You will understand when you get there."

Jai gulped down the last bite of her sandwich.

"I don't know if I can make it."

Although her stomach was full, the muscles in her legs continued to clench and burn.

"You'll be able to rest soon, Jai, but you must move on. You can do it."

Jai gazed at the fallen star as it burned softly and inhaled one last breath of its beautiful fragrance.

"You know, you remind me of my Mom in ways."

"Why, thank you, Dear. That's quite a compliment."

"Do you know her?"

"Yes. In fact, you look just like her. Especially your eyes."

Jai's heart raced, excited and hopeful.

"Does she... come around here?"

The Fire paused in a sweet sort of way.

"You are to make this Journey on your own, Jai."

"Yeah, I know. I was just hoping that maybe I'd run into her somehow, I mean... since you know her."

Again, the faint pulse of drums reverberated through the sky. Jai tilted her head, listening. The flames danced in unison with the beat. And as quickly as it came, the song vanished into hushed silence.

"Your journey is calling you, Jai," said the Fire.

She carefully placed the seeds in her front pocket.

"Yeah, I guess it's time for me to go. Thanks for everything."

"You are welcome, Jai. Keep shining."

"Thanks. You too."

"You can be certain of that, Dear."

With renewed determination, Jai fixed her gaze on the hills ahead and trudged on, thinking of her mother's eyes.

CHAPTER 10

Jai read the sign and scratched her head. She had just slogged up another demanding peak. Taking a deep breath, she read it again. The message made no sense, but at least she was on the final hill. A vast desert sprawled out below, ancient carpets of beige and pink sand stretched across endless terrain, sprinkled with occasional clusters of vibrant green plants. A lone tree stood in the distance, its leaves shimmering in the sun. Beyond that, three magnificent mountains shot boldly from the horizon's edge.

Jai paused for a few minutes—hoping to regain some strength. It didn't work. Exhausted, she commanded her legs to continue walking—she had to get to that tree. The night was fast approaching and she needed a place to rest. Her shins felt like rubber bands, ready to pop. Regardless, an unusually bright fragrance attracted her. It seemed to be coming from the distant tree. The mysterious scent coaxed, soothed and uplifted her all at once.

Jai made her way across the desert under the darkening sky. All was still. She was about 100 yards from the tree when a chorus of disturbing laughter squealed in the distance. It seemed to be coming from behind her. The cackles grew louder, and Jai had a growing suspicion she was being followed. Picking up her pace, she glanced nervously over her shoulder. There, in the gray of dusk, she saw a pack of spotted hyenas trotting towards her, their eyes glowing. Jai's stomach flipped. She'd heard about hyenas from kids at school—especially the bone-breaking strength of their jaws. Even though they were known to be scavengers, they were also hunters—good ones. They could take down lions, not to mention girls. And they were gaining on her.

In a flash, Jai bolted towards the tree. The hyenas dashed in response. Instantly, they were at her heels. She could hear them panting, their hot breath stinking of rotten meat. The tree was just paces away. A set of jaws chomped at the back of her leg but missed. With all the strength she had left, Jai leapt towards the lowest branch. In that moment, the Leaf slipped from her pocket, changed into a huge eagle and lunged directly into the pack while she hoisted herself up to safety. The Leaf, however, was caught. The hyenas were now fighting over it, playing tug-of-war as it changed from an eagle to a hawk, to a condor, even a vulture. The pack drooled and chortled as feathers flew into the air.

"STOP!!!" Jai screamed.

The hyenas growled as they chomped into the Leaf, wildly shaking their heads to and fro, flinging the bird in all directions.

Desperate, Jai grabbed a nearby branch. It bent easily enough. She thought to use it as some sort of whip to try to scare the pack away. But something was weighing it down. Lemons! She was in a lemon tree.

Jai quickly plucked a fruit and aimed for one of the hyenas. He didn't have a chance. Jai was the best baseball pitcher in her school. She squinted through the dusk and hurled a fireball pitch directly at the hyena's nose. It was a clean shot. The lemon blasted into his muzzle and detonated, spurting juice everywhere. Jai was unrelenting. She pummeled her assailant with strike after strike. Wailing in pain, lemon juice burning its eyes, the hyena released the bird and ran away. One down. More torpedo pitches and another hyena winced loudly and raced off. Jai hurled lemon after lemon with laser precision. Soon, the entire pack fled. Clinging to the tree, her heart pounding, she listened as an echo of menacing squeals trailed off in the distance.

"You okay?" she asked, peering at the hawk on the ground below.

The bird rustled its feathers and flew up to her branch. Jai carefully inspected the hawk for bites. Surprisingly, it didn't seem hurt. She lovingly stroked its feathers.

"We better sleep up here tonight!"

The hawk nodded, gave her affectionate peck and hopped

up to a branch above her head, eager to stand guard.

Jai had never slept in a tree before. She wasn't really sure how to do it. It was uncomfortable, but she managed to wedge her body between the center of the tree and a web of tangled branches at her back. At first she was too anxious to sleep. The pack could return at any moment. Not only that, the knots on the branches kept poking her in the ribs. Too tired to do anything else, she eventually drifted off to sleep.

Early the next morning, she bolted awake—a hyena was waiting directly below her.

Jai immediately grabbed a lemon and took aim.

"Please don't hit me."

It never occurred to her that hyenas could talk. She looked closely into the animal's eyes and was surprised to see a genuine softness there.

"We hyenas are not understood, Jai. Just as there are those who don't understand you."

"How do you know my name?"

"The Water Trees sent me."

"They sent YOU?!"

"We meant you no harm."

"Well, you could have fooled me!" Jai adjusted herself cautiously on her branch.

The hyena smiled gently. "The pack came to protect the land here. We've heard about humans and their destructive ways."

"I'm human, but that doesn't make me destructive! Couldn't they have just asked me what I was doing here and not attack me?"

"That's a good point, Jai. Humans would do well to consider the same thing. The Water Trees contacted us last night. We now understand that you are different and mean no harm. You are free to roam here. We wish you well." And with that, the hyena gently trotted away.

This was nothing like what Jai had heard about hyenas.

The morning sun continued to rise. Jai stretched and noticed two objects on a branch near her head, an unusual looking—clump—of something—like a bundle, and a bird's nest. The hawk, in the meantime, continued to stand guard nearby, looking fierce as ever.

"I wonder what that is," she said to the bird, inspecting the clump.

"Ahhhh, young lady, it is for you!" answered a deep masculine voice.

Jai stopped. "Who said that?"

"Do not worry, young lady. It's just me."

She realized it was the Lemon Tree.

"Uh…I hope it's okay that we stayed here last night."

"But of course!" answered the tree. "We have been waiting for you. Now, go ahead—don't be shy. That is for you."

Jai reached towards the unusual bundle. It felt like old, soft leather.

"For me?"

"Indeed!"

As she retrieved the mysterious bundle, a single ray of early morning light fell upon the entire branch. She noticed something gleaming from the bird nest. Leaning towards it, Jai pulled a single threaded needle from the twigs. It was very thin, with an impossibly small hole at one end. Looking closely, she accidentally pulled the thread out from the hole.

"Aaaaahhh! You have found them!"

"You mean...this needle and thread?"

"Indeed!"

"What are they for?"

"You will see. Hop down! A new morning has arrived!"

"But what if the hyenas come back?"

"Ahhhhh, young lady, you have a powerful arm and excellent aim! They won't bother you again after that!"

"Are you sure?"

"Positive!"

Making sure not to drop the bundle or the needle, Jai quickly hopped down and stretched.

It was an odd thing to find a lemon tree in the middle of a desert, yet there it was—boasting an abundant crop of fruit.

The hawk morphed into a bright green macaw and flew to her shoulder. Cocking its blazing orange beak back and forth, it nodded with great enthusiasm.

Jai stared at the bundle in her hands. The macaw had other interests; it quickly hopped to a nearby branch and began pecking at a lemon.

"Hey, don't do that!" scolded a voice.

Startled, Jai noticed a very angry looking Stem. It was sitting dangerously close to the lemon being assaulted.

"Unruly thing!" chided the Stem.

"Now, now, be easy," replied the Lemon Tree. "These are our guests."

Jai quickly motioned for the macaw to get off the branch.

"No, no, it's okay," encouraged the Tree.

"No, it's NOT!" countered the Stem, annoyed. "I don't particularly feel like being pecked into mulch today, thank you very much!"

The macaw flew back to her shoulder, bobbing its head.

"Now, you *know* they don't mean any harm," said the Lemon Tree.

"Sorry," offered Jai.

"Well, you *are* first-timers, so all is forgiven," said the Stem still looking down its tiny nose at Jai and her Leaf.

"So, you must be the one going to *The Land of The Drum*," continued the Lemon Tree.

"Yeah, that's me."

"Mmmmmmmm," the Tree nodded. Its low, deep voice rumbled slowly.

Jai looked thoughtfully at The Tree, admiring its brilliant yellow lemons.

"Do people ever use your lemons for lemonade?"

"Why, yes. I especially like Earl, the old one with the braid. He's a very good man. I dream of him often."

"You dream about him, too? But you're a tree."

"Yes, young lady. I have noticed that."

"I, just, never really thought about trees dreaming."

"We all dream, one way or another."

"C'mon!" interrupted the Stem. "Aren't you going to open

it?"

"She will when she is ready," noted the Tree.

Jai slowly opened the bundle, revealing an ancient leather strap that had been sewn together into a large continuous loop. The weathered hide rested comfortably in her hands, soft, supple and unquestionably strong. A dazzling sun, sewn of countless golden seeds, had been masterfully stitched into the strap.

"This must be The Leather and The Sun!"

The seeds exuded a mysterious power, forming a round shining medallion that was flawless. Well, almost flawless. Jai noticed that three seeds were missing from the outermost edge of the Sun.

Jai felt a warm tingling in her front pocket. The seeds! The Fire had given her three seeds. And the Sun was missing three seeds.

"Now the *Eye of the Needle* sign makes sense," said Jai.

She knew what needed to be done. The only problem was that she had no experience sewing, other than the time her mom showed her in a dream. That was so many years ago. Regardless, she knew she would have to try.

Jai sat under the Lemon Tree and attempted to thread the needle with clumsy, undomesticated fervor. She held the needle and thread close to her eyes, wet the tip of the thread with her tongue and tried to force it through the impossibly small hole. It didn't work. She tried it again, only with more force. The thread defiantly refused to pass through the eye. She paused, took a breath, and tried again. The thread bounced off the needle.

"Ahhhh, young lady, you must be patient," encouraged the Lemon Tree.

"Nothing I'm doing works."

"You have to steady your hands. Try again."

Her hands were more controlled, but she still missed.

"You've steadied your hand, young lady, but now you must steady your mind."

Jai heaved a frustrated sigh and tried again and again. After a while, her mind started to drift. She thought about her dad and how *he* never sewed anything. Once he tore his jacket and patched it up with duct tape. She put down the needle and thread, thinking:

Ugh, this is hard. I don't want to do this anymore.

"WHAT?!" exclaimed the Stem, hearing her thought. "Didn't you read the sign? It said, 'Don't give up'!"

"I can't help it. This is hard! And I *did* give it my all!"

"*THAT'S* your 'all'? You have to really *mean* it, Jai! This is supposed to be a *Great* Adventure, remember? You have to be persistent! Really, how horribly dull—to try a couple of puny times and just give up. Very, very drab if you ask me. Why, if I had given up, I'd never have become a Stem at all!"

"Huh?"

"My Dear, you don't suppose one just *becomes* a Stem do you? It takes tremendous hard work to even get in, much less graduate."

"Get into where?"

"Why, *The Academy*, of course!"

"You went to school to become a Stem?"

"Not just any school," answered the Stem proudly, *"The Royal Academy."*

"Hmmm."

"Have you ever considered where a flower or a Leaf might be without us?"

Jai had no answer. Regardless, she was relieved to be thinking about something else.

"Let me ask you this," continued the Stem. "On a windy day, who keeps the leaves on the trees?"

Jai thought a moment. "Stems."

"And who makes sure that flowers can stand up?"

"Stems."

"And that's only the beginning. We learn those things during the first semester. It's a four-year program."

"Wow. What do you learn later on?"

"Things that would astound you, my dear."

"Like what?"

"Well, there's *Deciduous Trees 101*—a Master Class required for graduation. For that, we have to successfully let go of our leaves in the fall."

"What's so hard about that? I see you guys do that all the time."

"My dear, we're very fond of our leaves. It's not easy to let them go. Learning to graciously suffer this sort of separation isn't easy. And we do it year after year."

Jai never really thought about any of this before—how something so small could be so necessary in the bigger scheme of things, and the strength of character it took to do so. She looked at the Stem with a new respect.

"And," continued the Stem, "as any *Royal Academy* graduate will tell you: every new effort requires that you make at least 6.25 mistakes, but usually more than that."

"6.25? Why the decimal point?"

"We Stems are very precise."

"Oh."

"And as for *you*, learning to thread a needle for the first time requires that you make a minimum of 17 mistakes before getting it right, and you stopped at 14."

"Are you sure?"

"My dear, I'm a *Stem*! Of course I'm sure."

"You mean—I'm really that close to getting it?"

"Only if you keep trying. And *only* if you really mean it."

"Well, of course I do!"

Jai picked up the needle and thread with renewed vigor. Squinting with determination, she aimed the thread at the eye of the needle and, wouldn't you know, on her eighteenth try, the thread slipped right through the needle's eye.

"YES!" shouted Jai, jumping up, elated.

At that moment, the beat of a drum reverberated like a single clap of thunder across the sky. Jai could hear a man singing along. He sounded as if he was up in the heavens, yet the voice felt oddly familiar. In a flash, the music was gone.

"Ahhhhhh, young lady, you are indeed on a Great Adventure!" commented the Lemon Tree.

She reached into her pocket and retrieved the three golden seeds.

"How many mistakes do I need to make before I can actually sew them on?"

"I can't tell you that part," replied the Stem. "It all depends on how hard you try. The more sincerely you try, the closer you will get. Really, Jai, show some initiative."

"Ahhhhhh, just be patient, young lady," encouraged the Lemon Tree.

Jai sat back down and attempted to sew the golden seeds onto The Leather and The Sun. After accidentally pricking her finger eight times, dropping the needle twelve times, and poking The Leather in the wrong place twenty-two times, she finally made her first successful stitch in the exact place where the first golden seed was to be sewn in. The next stitch was a little easier, the next one even easier. The Lemon Tree and the Stem looked on approvingly.

Soon, Jai was on the last of the three seeds. Upon completing the final stitch, without warning, the Sun on the leather began to glow, becoming brighter and brighter. Startled, Jai dropped the leather from her hands. As it hit the ground, an enormous, blinding stream of light exploded out from the Sun's center, hurtling all the way across the Sky. As quickly as the beam shot out, it vanished back into the seeds, which now glowed orange.

"What was THAT?" asked Jai, frightened.

"*That*, young lady, was the BRIGHTEST light I have ever seen!" answered the Lemon Tree.

Jai looked up at the Stem, wide-eyed.

"Did you learn anything about this at *The Royal Academy*?"

"Uh, not really," stammered the Stem. "But one thing's for sure: *Whatever* that was, it *meant* it!"

CHAPTER 11

"WHOA!!! Did you see that?!"

"See what, Billy?" Ms. Hanks was busy scribbling copious amounts of forgettable facts up on the chalkboard.

"That flash of light!"

Everyone thought Billy was up to his old antics. As it was, he already had to stay after school for detention three times that week. As far as Billy was concerned, it wasn't *his* fault that school was so slow and boring. Pranks were just a way of keeping himself entertained, especially with Jai being gone. Life just wasn't the same.

"I didn't see anything," yawned Natalie, admiring her latest nail polish.

Ms. Hanks slowly put down her chalk, and turned to gaze out the window. There wasn't a cloud in the sky. Everyone expected Billy to get scolded again for making trouble.

"I don't think there's a storm rolling in," noted Ms. Hanks. "It's probably just Jai."

"JAI?!" exclaimed the class in unison.

"Yes Jai." Ms. Hanks resumed scribbling on the chalkboard.

Billy's eyes popped.

"Well, what ABOUT Jai? I mean, did she just blow up or

something? What was that flash?"

"No, Billy, she didn't blow up. But I'd say it's time for us to start having a daily window check."

"Window check?"

"Indeed. Billy, that's your new assignment. You're to look out the window every morning when I tell you to."

"For real?" Billy peered suspiciously at Ms. Hanks. He just couldn't believe that a teacher, *any* teacher, would actually *want* him to stare out the window during class.

Ms. Hanks' keen eyes narrowed towards him, her right eyebrow shot up with authority. He felt the hairs stand up on the back of his neck.

"Yes, Billy. For real."

"Why can't *I* do it?" whined Robert Peabody Smith III.

"No, Ms. Hanks, can't I do it?" pleaded Jeffrey Hammersfield, who *still* had a secret crush on Jai after two and a half years. It didn't even matter to him that Jai was better than him at sports.

"Please, Ms. Hanks, pick me," pleaded Patrice Zonaire, whose crushes *still* changed all the time. In fact, just the week before, he had had a *major* crush on Jai. But as soon as she plucked her Leaf, he decided to go for someone more local.

"Obviously, with my fine eye for detail, I'm the best one for this," concluded Natalie, adjusting her brand new Geechee necklace.

"No," replied Ms. Hanks firmly. "This is Billy's job."

"Why does Billy get to do it?" complained Jeffrey.

"Because he's the only one who can see it."

Everyone in class looked at each other, confused.

"Um, Ms. Hanks? What...exactly...am I looking for?" asked Billy.

"Why, that which the others can't! The only way the class will be able to see it is if you see it first, Billy."

"See *what* first?"

"You'll know." A slight grin traced across her lips.

"But—"

"Everything in its time, Billy," interrupted Ms. Hanks. "And, class, there's no use in feeling jealous that Billy gets to do this. Trust me, it's *because* he can see it that you will, too. Nobody will miss out. That's just how it works. Now, everybody get your literature books out."

"How *what* works?" asked Robert Peabody Smith III.

"Robert, we've moved on to literature," Ms. Hanks stated firmly.

Everyone opened their books, wildly exchanging looks while pretending to look at the pages. No one said a word.

How can you talk about anything as boring as literature right now? thought Billy, gazing out the window.

"BILLY!" shot Ms. Hanks' voice, quick and sharp as the red pencils on her desk. "Did I say it was time for you to look out the window?"

"No, Ms. Hanks."

"I'll let you know when," she assured him.

Billy looked down at his book, bewildered, but incredibly excited just the same. *Wow, Jai,* he thought, *what are you up to?*

CHAPTER 12

The Leather and The Sun rested unassumingly on the ground while Jai, the macaw, The Lemon Tree and the Stem all watched it with startled respect. It took a while for the seeds of the Sun to cool from bright orange to gold. For the moment, Jai dared not touch it. The air was so still you could hear a pin drop—or, in this case, a needle.

The distant sound of a beating drum suddenly broke the silence. Its pulse drifted across the sky—this time accompanied by a beautiful melody from an unknown voice. And then in an instant, it was gone.

"Ahhhhhh, young lady," noted the Lemon Tree, "an ancestor is singing to you. Do you hear?"

"Yeah, but I don't know what he's saying."

Soothed by the mysterious song, Jai suddenly grew tired. Her eyelids drooped heavily; her legs turned to lead.

"It's been a long day. I think I'll just..." She curled up beneath the Lemon Tree. "...rest here for a little while."

"Ahhhhhh, yes, that's a very good idea," said the Tree as Jai fell into a deep sleep.

"Hey, hey! Hello there!"

It was Earl, smiling and sporting an enormous pair of dark sunglasses.

"Hi. Am I dreaming?" asked Jai.

"Sure are! See, I told you you'd soon learn to tell the difference."

"Was that you singing?"

"Yep."

"What were you singing about?"

"It was a celebration song. You know, not many have been able to figure out how to sew those seeds onto The Leather and The Sun."

"Wow, I didn't know," she replied.

"It's true. The Leather and The Sun is very powerful, Jai. And it's a part of you now."

"A part of me?"

"Uh-huh. You fixed it with your own hands. So now it's a part of you."

"Hmm. Why are you wearing sunglasses?"

"Well, until you learn how to handle that beam of light, I thought it'd be a good idea."

"Did you see that, too?"

"Oh, me and everybody else for miles and miles," said Earl.

"Well, it scared me to death!"

"That's only because you don't know how to use it yet, and that's just what we're going to talk about next. First of all, you need to learn how to wear it."

"Wear it? I'm not going to wear that thing! What if the light shoots out and I explode or something?"

"That won't happen," Earl grinned, adjusting his sunglasses. "The Leather and The Sun is very, very old. It is to be treated with great respect, for it is powerful and will help you in many ways. You're on a brave journey. And, believe me, you'll need it. Truly, it's a gift."

Jai thought for a minute.

"That's what the Lemon Tree said too. And the Water Trees told me to be sure and use all the gifts that come my way. It's *that* kind of gift, right?"

"Sure is. Now, it's good that you fixed it yourself, because that way it has even more meaning for you. It's important to do things for yourself whenever you can. Now here's how you wear it."

Earl picked up The Leather and The Sun and placed the strap over Jai's head, draping it over her left shoulder so that it fell, like a banner, across her chest. The golden seeds of the Sun covered her heart. It was a perfect fit. Jai looked down at the golden Sun that gleamed majestically over her heart. She instantly felt light and strong, and oddly royal.

"Are you *sure* I won't explode or anything?"

"Positive. Always wear the Sun over your heart. It will protect you and guide the way, especially in the dark."

"The dark?"

"Uh-huh. But before we go any further, you better wear these." Earl handed her a pair of sunglasses.

"Okay, here's what you do. Simply touch the center of the Sun with one of your fingers."

"Are you sure?" asked Jai, as she put on the glasses and cautiously looked down at the beaded disc.

"I'm sure."

"What if I evaporate?"

"You won't."

"Well... okay..." Jai decided that since she was dreaming, even if she *did* blow up she'd still wake up in one piece. Hopefully.

With great hesitation, she pressed her index finger on the center of the beaded Sun. An enormous shaft of light immediately shot out with such force that it knocked her off her feet. The brilliant light sliced chaotically through the air as she tumbled to the ground.

"Help!" cried Jai as the light continued to stream unabated from her chest.

"Now, now, it's okay," assured Earl. "Remember, The Leather and The Sun are a part of you."

"A part of me?" she screamed, "This thing's going to kill me! Turn it off! Turn it off!"

"Oh, I can't," answered the old man. "Only you can do that."

"WHAT?!!!"

"Just touch the center of the Sun again. You'll see."

At that moment, amidst her panic, Jai heard the pulse of drums beating in the distance. A wave of calmness washed over her. Her heartbeat slowed, matching the rhythm of the drumbeat. She closed her eyes and touched the Sun with her finger. Instantly, the beam vanished back into the disc of golden beads.

"And *that*," concluded Earl while taking off his sunglasses, "is how you turn it on and off."

"You mean, I can control it?" asked Jai, astonished.

"Sure can! Like I said, you're the *only* one who can. It's a part of you, so it's important that you know how to use it."

"But what if it shoots out and hurts someone?"

"Well, you're still just getting started, so the power of it frightens you a bit. Just remember that The Leather and The Sun can never hurt anyone when it's used in a good way. It has been given to you for a reason, Jai—trust that. For now, what's important is that you know how to wear it, and how to turn it on and off. Just think of it as a very special flashlight. Got it?" Earl gave Jai a mischievous wink.

"Got it," said Jai.

Although still dreaming, she suddenly felt exhausted. Jai tried to stay awake, but soon drifted off to sleep as Earl made himself a fresh glass of lemonade.

"OUCH!"

The macaw was pecking at Jai's head. She woke to find herself back under the Lemon Tree, feeling rested and refreshed. As she stood up and stretched, she noticed that the sun was about to set.

"Wow, I just had an amazing dream."

"Ahhhhhhh, young lady, that is a good thing," replied the Lemon Tree. "Did you learn anything new?"

"I'll say. Earl taught me how to use The Leather and The Sun. I'm supposed to wear it and use it like a flashlight!"

"Hmmmm," replied the Lemon Tree and the Stem in unison.

"Here, I'll show you."

Jai picked up The Leather and The Sun and put it on as Earl had instructed. Even in the fading light of dusk, its thousand golden seeds shined lustrously over her heart.

"Ahhhhhhh, it is beeeautiful," commented the Lemon Tree.

"Quite impressive," added the Stem.

Just then Jai noticed a small sign behind the Lemon Tree. It read:

GO TO THE MOUNTAINS
DEEP IN THE NIGHT.
CLIMB FOR THREE DAYS
AND WALK ON THE LIGHT.

"Walk on the light?" repeated Jai to herself, scratching her head.

"Perhaps you should investigate a little further," offered the Lemon Tree.

Jai then spotted a second sign, behind the first. It was the shortest message thus far. It simply read:

Jai was even more perplexed.

The sun was sinking into the horizon. It was getting dark fast.

"Young lady, I think it's time for you to go," said the Lemon Tree.

"But it's night now. I won't be able to see anything or get anywhere."

The macaw jumped up onto Jai's shoulder and began pecking at her head again.

"OUCH! Is that necessary?"

"Apparently so," chided the Stem. "Didn't you say you were just taught how to use The Leather and The Sun?"

"Well, yes."

"So...*use it!*"

"Oh."

With the tip of her right index finger, Jai gently touched the center of the Sun. Immediately, an effulgent beam blasted out from the seeds. This time, however, Jai remained calm. The Stem squinted its eyes and ducked behind a branch, bending away from the light as if in a windstorm.

"It's okay, it won't hurt you," assured Jai, surprised to hear herself speak with such authority.

"Then TURN IT THE OTHER WAY!" shouted the Stem. "That thing's blinding me!"

"Oh, sorry."

Jai turned to face the mountains in the distance. The beam stretched like luminous taffy, reaching all the way across the landscape onto the most distant horizon.

"It really won't take you long to get there," assured the Lemon Tree, admiring the brilliant stream of light.

"But the mountains look like they're a million miles from here."

"Yes, that may be true..." said the Lemon Tree, "...but as it says on page five of *The Rule Book*..."

"I, uh, I only read the first couple of pages."

The Stem shook its tiny head in disbelief. "You're on a Great Adventure, and you didn't even read the entire *Rule Book*?"

"Well... I... uh... "

"On page five," continued the Lemon Tree, "it clearly states: 'When you know where you're going, you don't waste time.'"

"Oh."

"You know where you need to go, Jai. So it won't take long."

Jai stared at the colossal expanse between herself and the mountains in the distance. She gulped as she thought of wandering alone through that darkening abyss.

"Just keep walking," encouraged the Lemon Tree.

Those words reminded her of the Water Trees, which helped a little. She paused, touched the Sun with her finger, and the beam vanished again; its beads sparkled crimson orange and then darkened to a soft gold.

"What do I do when I get hungry?"

She didn't know if her Leaf would always bring her sandwiches.

"There will always be nuts and berries for you along the way," answered the Lemon Tree. "The plants will feed you. You'll know what to do. But it's always a good idea to collect extra nuts and berries in your pockets when you find them."

"That's it? Nuts and berries? The entire time?"

The Lemon Tree smiled.

"You will always have what you need. Don't worry."

Jai thought about her dad. His snacks were the best in the neighborhood. In comparison, nuts and berries just didn't cut it. A knot rose in her throat. She wondered if she'd ever see him again.

"Aahhhhhh, you'll be fine, young lady. But now it really is time for you to go."

The Lemon Tree was right. The night had wasted no time in arriving. Nature had clearly read page five, or maybe even written it. Jai double-knotted her shoelaces and took a deep breath.

"Thanks for everything, you guys."

"You are most welcome!" answered the Lemon Tree.

"A pleasure," added the Stem.

Jai turned to face the mountains, touched the Sun with her finger, and followed the light that blasted forth from the seeds. The dazzling beam teetered slightly as she walked. The macaw remained perched tightly on her shoulder. Thus, amidst the dark blue and gray of dusk, a mysterious stream of light wobbled its way across the desert.

CHAPTER 13

As Jai continued her venture into the night, her thoughts often drifted to home. She missed hearing the high squeak of the oven opening and closing when her dad baked desserts after work. He had taught himself how to bake when she was three years old. At first the results were always the same: charcoal on a plate. But he soon got the hang of it. She missed devouring after-school snacks with Billy before racing to The Water Tree Grove.

The cool desert night air kept her awake. The macaw nestled against the side of her neck and dozed. Amidst the vast expanse of the desert, Jai felt incredibly small. She thought about her mom. It felt like forever since she'd seen her in a dream. Jai missed how they would sing and dance together, crack jokes and ride bicycles—all as she slept. She never felt envious of other kids whose mothers were still living. After all, she still *did* have a mom. But that night, alone under the gigantic sky, she longed to reach out and hold her mother's hand, just like she'd seen other kids do.

She tried to comfort herself by thinking about the Water Trees, but that made her feel even worse. Everything and everyone she loved was so far away. Her heart grew heavy and her feet began to drag. She considered turning around. Maybe she'd sleep up in the Lemon Tree for a second night. Her thoughts were soon interrupted however—not by a mosquito, or by drums, but by the very cosmos itself.

The first star of the night had come out quietly, high above her head. It began to sing. Gentle melodies intertwined as more and more stars appeared, adding to the chorus. Soon thousands of stars bejeweled the blue-black sky. From horizon to horizon, glorious bell-like melodies twinkled from each speck of light. The entire galaxy had come to keep her company—singing songs of welcome and reassurance. Such mysterious beauty and radiance erased all her fears. And, in that moment, everything— the stars, the endless expanse of sand—all of creation, felt like an old friend. A tingle went down Jai's spine and her entire body felt infused with an extraordinary energy. Awestruck, she walked forth with sure and quiet steps.

And, true to page five of *The Rule Book*, it really *didn't* take that long to reach the mountains. It was still dark when she arrived. The night cloaked the mountains before her; yet she could feel their enormous presence. Exhausted, Jai settled down under a large sycamore tree.

"I think this is a good spot to rest," she informed the macaw.

The bird nodded in agreement.

Jai turned off the beam, curled up under the tree, and fell asleep. Meanwhile, the macaw flew up to the lowest branch, morphed into an enormous falcon with fierce black eyes, and stood guard over Jai as she slept.

Morning came quickly. Ribbons of fog draped lazily across

the landscape. The sunrise created hues of translucent rose, gold and orange that swept across the terrain. Groggy, Jai yawned and stretched. The falcon echoed her yawn and shrugged its feathers. As Jai sat to look up she was stunned.

Three impossibly gigantic mountains towered before her. She'd never seen anything so commanding and massive in all her life. She tilted her head up, and up, and up again, as she followed the slope of each mountain to its crest, which peaked out of the clouds like three royal crowns. Two of the peaks were covered in snow but the tallest peak looked barren.

Meanwhile, the falcon swooped from its branch and flew to a nearby sign that Jai had not yet seen.

The sign was clearly pointing to the highest mountain. Jai noticed the beginning of a path only a short trek away.

Jai and the falcon peered at each other.

"Really? Said Jai, "A sign that actually makes sense the first time you read it?"

The falcon screeched in agreement and morphed back into a Leaf.

"OK, here we go then."

Jai tucked the Leaf into her back pocket and headed for the trail.

Over the next three days she climbed steep bluffs, walked up rocky paths, and kicked her way through tough underbrush.

The Leaf chose to morph into a red robin. It darted from tree to tree, all the while carefully keeping pace with its companion. And just as the Lemon Tree had predicted, there was plenty to eat. Jai picked a variety of sweet ripe berries and nuts that grew in abundance on the mountain. Whenever she picked something that wasn't good to eat, the robin would swoop down and peck her on the head. She learned quickly. The mountain fed her well and provided her with clean water from nearby streams. Jai *did* ask her Leaf for a sandwich a few times. The bird replied by landing on yet another ripe berry bush or a tree heavy with nuts. She would stuff her pockets and continue climbing. Truly, this was the most effortless part of her journey thus far. At one point, Jai even wondered if maybe the hardest part of her Adventure was over.

Despite the colossal height of the great mountain, she was making remarkable time and didn't even feel tired. In some mysterious way, Jai felt like the mountain itself was carrying her as she climbed. The higher she went, the easier it became.

At one point, when she encountered a particularly steep bluff, she reached straight up, gripped a smooth stone on the ledge above her head and, with a single effortless move, pulled herself up to the next level. She rolled onto her back, laughing at how surprisingly easy it had been for her. But when she looked up she was shocked at what she saw—or, rather, didn't see. There was no more mountain! She had reached the top!

Jai jumped up and down and offered the bird a high-five, but it had never learned about high-fives. As she looked around the mountaintop, she found herself immersed in perfect silence, a pristine stillness like she had never experienced before. Jai had figured it'd be windy up on the mountain—just as Ms. Hanks had described in science class. But all was quiet. It reminded her of the perfection of a newly opened jar of peanut butter—that exceptional moment enjoyed only once in a jar's life, a smooth calm surface, completely unblemished by an intruding knife or spoon.

Jai stood as silent as the mountain itself, enjoying an inner serenity she had never known. A rich, warm sensation delighted every cell of her body. Breathing softly, she gazed at the terrain before her. The royal crown of the mountain was surprisingly flat. Fields of lush green moss were punctuated by enormous boulders, rounded over time. Several banana trees stood in the distance, stout and brimming with fruit. Jai turned to the robin; it was pecking at some moss near her feet.

"I didn't know fruit trees could grow all the way up here!"

The robin nodded, morphed into an enormous eagle, and boldly took to the sky.

Jai was making her way to pick a banana, when she noticed a small sign nestled in a nearby tuft of moss. It read:

When she gazed out beyond the sign, her knees went soft and her jaw dropped.

The Nose Bleed Section at the pool was NOTHING compared to this. From the Top of the World, the entire planet sprawled out like a great quilt—an endless mosaic brimming with textures and patterns, and blue squiggly lines of rivers zig-zagging throughout.

Just then, the eagle swooped down before her and quickly morphed into the Leaf. Jai flipped it over, map-side-up.

"WHOΛΛΛ!"

There, in her hands, gleamed an entire world unto itself. The map revealed clouds and mountains, rivers and canyons, oceans and islands and all sorts of roads. Endless paths with intersecting lines wove throughout the Leaf. Along the paths Jai saw forests and hills covered with flowers. She noticed caves, various animals, and ancient, sacred domes of sculpted clay. There were sparkling waterfalls and rainbows connecting one ocean to the next. There was even a field comprised entirely of what looked like white feathers.

Jai gazed back at the world below. Everything she saw was on that map, only masterfully displayed in detailed miniature.

And yet, an entire half of the map still remained empty.

Jai took a second glance at the Top of the World sign and was so stunned she had to remind herself to breathe. The Leaf dropped from her hands, morphed back into an eagle and landed on the sign. To her amazement, the sign's message had changed.

Jai peered out over the world—past several mountain ranges, beyond a very dense blotch of a forest, many fields, and across an enormous turquoise ocean that sparkled in the sun. From this height, she could even see the slight curve of the earth on the horizon line of the water. The ocean seemed impossibly far away. Squinting, she detected an extremely small speck amidst the glistening sea.

I wonder if that's where I'm going, Jai thought.

She walked closer to the edge of the mountain, hoping to see more clearly. On her way, she saw a second sign. It read:

Jai looked out over the edge. To her surprise, the far side of the mountain shot straight down to the ground, thousands of feet below. There was no way to climb down from that side. Jai walked back to where she first reached the mountain top and froze. The very path she had followed was gone, a flat—and hopelessly steep—rock wall had taken its place. Jai was now surrounded on every side by what had become a perilous cliff.

Panic-stricken, she noticed yet another sign dangling precariously at the cliff's edge. It read:

Jai stood silent. The eagle landed next to her feet, transformed into a blue jay, and began peeling a banana with its beak. Looking out over the endless horizon from the Top of the World, Jai asked,

"How do we get down from here?"

The blue jay tilted its head for a moment and resumed working on the banana. Jai took a deep breath and decided to investigate. After exploring the Top of the World, it was easy to see that the only way to get down was *straight* down. Frightened, she returned to the bird; it was now enjoying a perfectly unpeeled banana.

"What are we going to do?"

The blue jay ate half the banana, looked up at Jai and morphed back into the Leaf.

Jai sat down on a mound of moss next to the Leaf and picked up the remaining half. Taking slow deliberate bites, she studied the map but it offered no clues to an escape.

She thought back to her last day at the Grove. The Stem had asked her,

"What do you do if you feel stuck?"

"Ask for help!" Jai answered aloud.

Another memory zoomed in her brain. The Eldest Tree had said that all Great Adventures include talking to the Sky. Jai figured *heh, why not try both at once?*

She'd never talked to the sky before. Jai sat up straight, as Ms. Hanks had taught, cleared her throat, and gazed up at the infinite expanse.

"Um. Excuse me, but I'm stuck up here. Could you please help me get back down?"

No answer.

Maybe it didn't hear me, she thought. Jai stood up, waved her arms to the heavens and shouted:

"EXCUSE ME. WHAT DO I DO NOW?"

Silence.

Jai sat back down.

"Maybe I didn't mean it enough."

Again she stood up, flailed her arms and screamed: "**I NEED HELP!!! I DON'T KNOW HOW TO GET BACK DOWN FROM—OUCH!**"

The Mosquito had bitten her sharply on the arm.

"Alright, alright, you don't need to make so much noise!" scolded the Mosquito. "The Top of the World is supposed to be a peaceful place, you know!"

"Why do you always have to BITE me?" said Jai, startled

and annoyed.

"Why is biting you the only way to get your ATTENTION? And *must* you continue to shout?"

Jai scratched her mosquito bite.

"I wanted to be sure the Sky could hear me."

"Honey, EVERYONE could hear you. Now, what does it say on page one of *The Rule Book*?! Even *you* read that much, as I recall."

Jai paused, grinning sheepishly. "It says to continue being patient."

"Well, in your case, why don't you START by being patient? The Sky will always hear you, so you don't have to scream about it! Besides, it could tell you *meant* it the first time you asked. As long as you're sincere, you're heard."

"Oh."

"So you're wondering how to get down from here?"

"Yes."

"Well, that's easy. Just use The Leather and The Sun."

Jai looked down at the golden seeds that gleamed softly over her heart.

"Does it turn into some kind of parachute?"

"Better than that! But first, let's start with the basics. You need a walking lesson, Jai."

"I already know how to walk!"

"Not on light, you don't."

"On light? Is that what that sign meant? You mean, you can really walk on light?"

"No, *you* can walk on light. You know the beam from The

Leather and The Sun? You can walk on it."

Amazed, Jai looked down at the magical leather strap that was draped across her chest.

"Now that you know how to turn it on and off, you're ready to learn how to use it. Remember, The Leather and The Sun are a part of you."

"Is it going to help me get down from here?"

"It's the ONLY way for you to get down from here. So let's get to work. It would have helped if you'd read page six of *The Rule Book*."

"Well, you know I haven't, so you might as well tell me what it said."

The Mosquito paused. "You know, when you go on a Great Adventure, you're supposed to come prepared, Jai."

"Seriously?" Jai scratched her mosquito bite, annoyed. "Ok, I'm sorry! There's nothing I can do about that now but learn from here."

"Hmmmm, you have a point," replied the Mosquito. "Okay then, on page six it clearly states: 'You must let the light support you.'"

"Support me? How?"

"That's easy. By trusting."

"Trusting?"

"Believe me, that light will become as solid as a sidewalk if you trust it to support you. That's part of the rules. Get it?"

"No."

"Well, you will."

The Mosquito zipped across the mountaintop, stopping by

one of the banana trees.

"Okay. First step: Touch the Sun with one of your fingers and aim the beam up here to this tree."

Jai did as instructed, and immediately a light blasted from the Sun, across the field, landing exactly on the tree. All of the branches, the bananas, and even the Mosquito glistened in its effulgence.

"Good aim," noted the Mosquito.

"Well, I *am* a girl," said Jai, "Now what?"

"Keep the light on and place The Leather and The Sun on the ground, facing the tree."

Jai took off the leather strap and laid it on the moss before her. The light beam continued to pour from the golden seeds, streaming up through the air onto the banana tree like a shimmering golden ribbon.

"Good. Now walk on it."

"Walk on it? Just like that?"

"Yes, walk on it."

Jai looked skeptically at the Mosquito. "Why don't YOU walk on it?"

"Well, if you insist."

The Mosquito hopped up and down all along the light—thoroughly delighted. It slid, skipped, and jumped back and forth. Eventually, it leapt off the beam and hovered next to Jai's ear, buzzing ecstatically.

"Okay," panted the Mosquito, "your turn."

"That's not fair! You don't weigh anything. One step on that light, and I'll fall right through."

"Not if you trust it to hold you up," said the Mosquito.

"But—"

"But nothing. One has to first try in order to get anywhere. So go ahead."

Jai lifted her right foot and prepared to step onto the golden beam. As she lowered her foot it went right through the light, landing firmly on the moss below.

"See?" insisted Jai.

"See what? That you're not concentrating? Yes, I can see that very clearly!"

"Well, what am I supposed to concentrate on?"

Jai was frustrated. *Mosquitos were always annoying enough as it was. This was a whole other level.*

"Do you want my help or not?" snapped the insect, hearing that thought.

Jai smirked.

"Yes."

"Better. Now, listen, Jai. You've got to trust—trust that the light will support you so you can walk on it."

"Okay, I'll try the other foot."

She lowered her left foot, and again it went straight through the light, landing on the ground.

"Ugh."

"Look," explained the Mosquito, "just because you're not used to thinking of light as something you walk on, that doesn't mean it can't be done."

"So what do I do?"

"Simple. Think that it's easy to do. Think to yourself that

walking on light is the most natural thing in the world, because, after all, it is."

"But what if I don't think that way?"

The Mosquito put its hand on its hip, so to speak, hovering near a banana.

"My Dear, it's time to stop being so boring and decide to change your mind."

"I'm not boring!" Jai defiantly put *her* hand on *her* hip.

"Well, answer me this then," countered the Mosquito. "Do you want to be able to walk on the light or not?"

"Well, I think I *have* to be able to. It's the only way to get down from here."

"Exactly."

Jai stood silently, thinking. The Mosquito buzzed softly, waiting.

"Well, how do I change my mind?"

"Now, that's the first step. It's simple. You have to know that you don't know."

"Well I think that part's obvious," replied Jai dryly, swinging her foot through the light.

"But this part is critical. Some things you have assumed to be true are not true and other things you assume are impossible can actually be done. You must first accept that some of your thinking has been wrong before you can change it."

Jai decided to give it another try. With each step, her foot went directly through the light to the ground. Determined, she continued wading through the slanted beam, until she stopped midway. The light was now up to her waist.

"This isn't working."

"That's because you think you're the one who's doing the work," observed the Mosquito.

"I'm going to be stuck up here forever," she sighed, feeling a little sorry for herself.

"Look, Jai, we in the insect world understand that even though we fly, there's always something greater than us that's helping us to do so. It looks like we're doing it all, but we're not. The same holds true for you."

"How do you know?"

"*You* have *The Rule Book*; *we* have the *Official Aerial Insect Flight Manual*."

The Mosquito took out a tiny book from under its wing and flipped through the pages, mumbling to itself.

"Let's see, *Navigational Techniques*? No, that's not it. Okay, here it is: 'All things move by a power greater than themselves— even humans who don't think so.' That includes *you*, Jai."

She stared again at the beam of light.

"I still don't know how I can stand on that thing. It's like I'd have to be made of helium, and I'm not."

"All you have to do is change the way you think. And you've already experienced what this is saying. How do you think you got up to the top of this mountain so quickly? Do you really think that was all *you*?"

The Mosquito was right. She *had* wondered about that.

"So...that power your manual talks about, *that's* how I made it up here so fast?"

"Absolutely. Nothing can move without it."

"Hmmmm."

Jai thought about the Stems. Maybe it was just like they teach at *The Royal Academy*, that whenever you try something new, a certain number of flops are required in order to get it right—as long as you don't give up. And the *Rule Book* said to always listen to Stems—so that meant it was possible.

She slowly raised her foot and declared with all her heart, "I have all of the help I need. That power is in me, too. I really *mean* it!"

Her foot stepped right through the light onto the ground below, just like before. Only this time, she chose not to feel discouraged. After all, she hadn't tried it that many times, and there wasn't a Stem around to tell her how many mistakes it would take. She tried it again. Nothing. Another time. Nothing. Flop after flop. But her thinking had changed; she *knew* she'd get it eventually. After all, Stems are *always* right. She just had to keep trying. The entire day went by with no victory in sight, but she refused to give in to disappointment. With every failure, she felt one step closer.

Jai remained on the mountaintop for days, trying again and again to step onto the light. At night, the beam of light illumined her efforts. Sleep evaded her and she took only a few short breaks to eat some of the remaining berries and nuts in her pocket. With every attempt, she'd raise her foot and say to herself, *This could be it!* The Mosquito nodded heartily in agreement each time.

Late one afternoon as the shadows grew long, Jai glanced at the Mosquito and asked, "Hey, are you keeping count of how many tries this makes?"

"Not really."

Jai eyed the sinking sun but remained thoroughly unshakable in her resolve.

This could be it.

She placed her foot on the light and froze in shock; it felt solid—like wood! Flabbergasted, she looked up at the Mosquito, buzzing with pride.

"Now you've got it, Jai! Go ahead, get the other foot up there, too."

She focused on the power she now felt assisting her and stepped onto the light with both feet.

"WOW! I'm on it! I'm really doing it!"

"How does it feel?"

"Weird. I mean, GREAT! This is FUN!!!"

"Go ahead. Walk!"

Jai cautiously inched her way across the light, her arms waving chaotically, like she was balancing on a tight rope.

"You're not going to fall, Jai. Just relax."

It didn't take her long to get the hang of it. Soon Jai was zooming back and forth on the luminous ribbon; jumping, skipping, and sliding.

"Hey, can I play soccer on this thing?" she asked while whizzing past the Mosquito.

"I don't see why not."

She tried all sorts of variations: sliding on one foot at a time, jumping as far as she could and landing on one foot, then the other. She was about to try a handstand when, without warning, the sound of Drums filled the air. The rhythm was soothing, joyous and triumphant all at the same time. And then, as quickly as it came, it vanished.

Jai stood motionless on the light, waiting to hear more.

"Well, that's enough for today," noted the Mosquito.

"But—"

"Hop down, Jai."

Jai jumped off the light. It was early evening and the sun was now very low in the enormous sky. She walked over to The Leather and The Sun, and turned the beam off with her finger.

"Come and take a seat, Jai. The show's about to begin."

Watching sunsets from the Top of the World had become one of Jai's all-time favorite activities. Every evening was different, each a glorious masterpiece.

She sat down on a tuft of moss and watched as rays of gold, pink and orange draped the entire earth like a blanket. Several flocks of birds glided homeward across the sky as pillow-like clouds blazed bright yellow along the horizon. Then all grew quiet and still. Neither breeze nor animal stirred. Amidst the soft glow of dusk, some colors dimmed, others brightened—immersing everything far below in translucent hues of pink, turquoise and purple.

Just as the sun dipped below the horizon Jai heard it whisper, in a deep grandfatherly tone, "See you tomorrow." And then it was gone. Ever generous, it sent a final parting gift: brilliant rays of magenta and orange shot from the edge of the horizon, while emblazoned clouds hung low in the western sky. The entire spectacle slowly dimmed to a grayish purple with hints of dull amber. Soon the entire dome of the Sky darkened to lapis blue.

One by one, tiny pinheads of light appeared in the heavens, flickering softly. Completely at peace, Jai softly yawned as each star began to sing—serenading the earth with soothing lullabies. And then, the entire cosmos, which had been waiting patiently behind daytime's curtain, took center stage. As the nocturnal concert began, endless layers of melodies twinkled throughout the heavens, lulling Jai into a deep sleep.

When she rolled over, it seemed as if the ground below her had shifted. She suddenly felt the weight of her lower legs and shoes swinging from her knees.

"YIKES!"

Jai found herself sitting on top of a 100-foot telephone pole, swaying frantically in the midst of a horrendous windstorm.

"Hey up there!" shouted a voice.

It was Earl. He looked like a small dot with a single braid blowing in the wind. In fact, he was standing near the foot of the pole, casually eating a banana.

"What am I doing up here?" screamed Jai.

"Just practicing," shouted Earl.

"For what?"

"For how to get out of tough situations."

"Is this a dream?"

"Yup."

"How do I get down from here?"

"Now Jai, you have to figure that part out for yourself."

Just then, a colossal wind whipped through the air. The telephone pole swayed ferociously.

"HELP!" Jai screamed, holding onto the top of the pole for dear life.

"Jai," shouted Earl, "you have everything you need to get yourself down from there. Use what you've learned."

Jai thought to herself as the telephone pole creaked back and forth.

"Am I supposed to use The Leather and The Sun?" she yelled.

"That'd be a good idea," shouted Earl.

Still careening through the air, Jai tried to think. She was feeling sick to her stomach.

I know how to walk on the light now, she woozily thought. *Maybe I can walk down off of here.*

She touched the center of the Sun with her finger. The light immediately shot out, creating a luminous arch that landed on the ground below. Jai quickly took off The Leather and The Sun, placed it on the top of the telephone pole and slid down the arch of light, landing—more like crashing—abruptly on the ground below.

"OUCH!"

"You okay?" asked Earl, helping her up.

"Yeah."

The storm suddenly vanished. Jai glanced up to the top of the telephone pole, where The Leather and The Sun continued to gleam.

"Great … now *it's* up there and *I'm* down here."

"Uh-huh. Sure looks that way," nodded Earl. "Of course, you haven't called it back to yourself yet."

"Called it back?"

"Yup. Go ahead and try it." Earl took another bite from the banana.

Jai did as Earl instructed.

"Um… please come back!"

Immediately, The Leather and The Sun stood at attention, leaped into the air, and landed softly at her feet.

"Wow, I didn't know it could do that."

You can never lose The Leather and The Sun, Jai. It'll always come to you when you call it. Got it?"

"Got it, but why are you telling me all this?" Jai yawned. She suddenly felt exhausted.

Earl gave a mischievous wink. "You rest now. After all, it takes a lot of energy to walk over the world."

Too tired from dreaming, she fell fast asleep.

CHAPTER 14

"Good morning!" sang the Mosquito as he zipped through the air.

"Good morning," yawned Jai, playfully swatting him away.

Jai woke up on the Top of the World just before daybreak. The lands below were coming to life—animals stirred, the wind gently picked up, and soon a pinpoint of light emerged from the eastern horizon. It quickly became a sliver, the Sky brightened and, the sun re-emerged, announcing the golden arrival of a brand new morning. Birds sang jubilant songs, plants sipped on fresh dew, and the entire world below was cleansed in the pure crisp air of dawn.

"You have a big day ahead of you, Jai, but first it's time for a nourishing breakfast!"

The Mosquito pushed an enormous plate of sliced bananas in front of her.

"I call it 'banana serenade.'" The Mosquito said, beaming with pride.

"I call it 'gross.'" Jai pushed the plate away. "I still feel kind of woozy from a dream I had last night."

"Well, just walk around a bit, and you'll feel better."

Jai got up, stretched, and took a short walk. Along the way, she noticed a sign. It read:

GO TO THE ISLAND
TRUST AND BELIEVE
HOP ON THE LIGHT—
AND LEAVE.

Jai returned to her bowl of "banana serenade" and enjoyed her breakfast while watching the sun's rays sweep their golden brilliance over the world below.

"I think I'm supposed to leave today," she told the Mosquito after taking the last bite.

"That's right, Jai. Do you have any questions before you go?"

"Yeah. Why do I keep hearing Drums?"

"Sorry, can't tell you."

"And where ARE they, anyway?"

"Can't tell you that either."

Jai eyed the Mosquito curiously.

"Why did you ask for questions if you won't answer them?"

"Well, ask the right question and you might get some answers!"

She thought a moment.

"Is there anything I should ask?"

"Now *that's* a good question! Yes, you should ask about

how to prepare yourself for leaving."

"Prepare myself?"

"Absolutely. You need to thank The Mountain before you go."

"I do?"

"Not everybody gets to come up here, you know."

"Uh. No, I didn't know that."

"Just past those banana trees, there's a very special place. You'll see."

Jai ventured past the trees. On the outskirts of a soft field of moss, two long brilliant blue feathers stuck out from the ground, bound together as a carefully arranged pair. Jai smiled. They were the exact same color as the Water Trees.

As she drew closer, Jai noticed that the two feathers were actually the largest pair of a series of feathers that encircled intricate etchings in the ground. At the center of the circle sat a large, gleaming, pink crystal, smooth and clear as polished glass, a magnificent royal jewel greeting the sky.

"Amazing, isn't it?" whispered the Mosquito, who was now buzzing softly by Jai's ear.

"What *is* this?" whispered Jai.

"This is the Heart of the Mountain."

"Wow."

"Go and say thank you, Jai."

"Thank you?"

"Yes. For letting you come here."

Slowly, she approached the pink crystal. It gleamed in the sunlight, emanating a soft, invigorating glow.

"I want to thank you for letting me come here," offered Jai.

The crystal radiated an extraordinary warmth and spoke in a calm, feminine voice. "You're welcome, Dear One."

"Offer a gift," whispered the Mosquito. "The Mountain's given you so much. It's only proper that you give something back."

Jai wondered what to do. She had already given her favorite stone to the Eldest Water Tree. Now, her only possessions were her Water Tree Leaf, some nuts she had harvested, and a useless stick of Perma-Lip.

"Don't give nuts!" buzzed the Mosquito, reading Jai's thought.

Jai slouched, embarrassed.

"I don't have anything," she confessed in a defeated whisper.

"Jai, GIVE SOMETHING!" commanded the Mosquito.

Looking apologetically at the Heart of the Mountain, she mumbled, "Excuse me, but would you care for some lipstick?"

"No, not the lipstick!" screamed the Mosquito, still trying to whisper.

Jai turned to the Mosquito buzzing frantically in her ear.

"You said 'Give a gift!' and that's all I have—LIPSTICK!" argued Jai in a loud whisper, now feeling defensive.

"No, Jai, not *that* kind of a gift!" said the Mosquito, shaking its head. "When you give something important, what counts is that you give from your *heart*, not just your pockets! I'm talking about the gift of yourself."

"Myself?"

"Haven't you learned a lot since coming up here?"

"Of course I have! I've learned a ton."

"Then give the gift of your *commitment*," stated the Mosquito with firm authority.

"My commitment?"

"This is a very special place, so you have to offer a very special kind of gift in return. The best gift you can give is to practice what you've been taught since you got here. Just choose one thing. Make a commitment to live it. Keep it simple."

This part of her Great Adventure wasn't as hard as learning to thread a needle for the first time, but it was close, Jai thought to herself. Flustered, she took a deep breath, remembering the Lemon Tree's instruction to steady her mind. Of all the amazing things she had learned on Top of the World, she wondered which one would make the best gift. It never occurred to her that a present could be something you can't even see or touch. After a long pause, she knelt down to the crystal and whispered,

"Thank you for giving so much. I commit to trusting the light to support me. I'll practice walking on it in a good way."

"Thank you, Dear One," answered the Heart of the Mountain. "Truly, that is a wonderful gift."

The Mosquito sighed a microscopic breath of relief.

And with that, it was time to go. Jai tucked her Water Tree Leaf in her back pocket and walked to the edge of the Top of the World. She peered out to a barely visible speck of an island near the horizon, her next destination.

"Do I point the light at the island?" she asked the Mosquito.

"You got it."

Jai squinted towards the almost imperceptible dot in the distance.

"That's all the way across the world. Will it reach that far?"

"Jai, it's pure light, it will go as far as it needs to—no problem."

"Well, here goes."

Jai touched the center of the golden seeds from The Leather and The Sun.

An enormous blast of dazzling light arced like a rainbow through the sky, all the way across the world, over mountains and forests and fields and part of an ocean, eventually seeming to reach its mark, far, far away.

"You need to leave The Leather and The Sun up here for now," instructed the Mosquito. "When you've reached the island, just call it back to you."

Jai gazed out over the world.

"And one more thing," added the Mosquito. "Make sure that you don't call The Leather and The Sun back to you until you've gotten all the way there."

"Okay, but why would I do that, anyway? That makes no sense."

"Trust me."

"Okay."

Jai peered at the earth miles below. It was a *long* way down.

"What if the wind knocks me off?" Jai gulped.

"Impossible. The Leather and The Sun will always protect

you. Just don't stop walking, and you'll be fine."

"How long will it take to get there?"

"Hardly any time at all. Walking on light tends to speed things up. You'll be there in a flash. Just remember to keep walking."

"Are you coming with me?"

"Nope, this is *your* Adventure."

Jai rechecked her back pocket for the Water Tree Leaf which was still tucked in tight, ready for the ride. She took a deep breath and stepped onto the light.

"Well, thanks again. Thanks for everything!"

"You're welcome," buzzed the Mosquito as it zipped excited circles from the mountain's edge. "Remember, Jai, keep walking!"

CHAPTER 15

Billy was absolutely bored out of his skull. Ms. Hanks had instructed him to look out the window at 10:12 sharp. It was finally 10:08 but the seconds dragged on and on. He fumbled with his pencil, drew pictures of racecars and soccer balls in the margins of his homework, but nothing helped to pass the time. Each agonizing second lingered as one infinity after another. Meanwhile, Ms. Hanks continued to scratch math equations on the chalkboard. Two minutes to go. Walter, the kid who sat next to Billy, thinking that no one was watching, picked his nose. One minute to go. Natalie swung her legs back and forth under her desk, her latest designer shoes barely skidding the floor. The ticking of the second hand seemed to grow louder as it passed the six and made its way around the bend to the long-awaited 12.

At last, it was 10:12. Ms. Hanks promptly turned around and gave Billy a subtle nod.

Eagerly, he scanned the sky beyond the window.

"Well, Billy?" asked Ms. Hanks, her right eyebrow arched slightly.

The rest of the class held their breath in anticipation.

"I don't see anything," he said disappointed. This was his

fifth day of "window patrol." He thought for sure today might be the day.

"Are you *sure?*" asked Ms. Hanks, her eyebrow now arching all the way towards her hairline.

"I don't see anything from my desk."

"Well, look closer."

Immediately, he sprang up and ran to the windows. Peering out, he saw nothing unusual. He pressed his nose to the glass to see higher in the sky.

"WOW! WHAT'S THAT?!!!"

Immediately, the entire class poured out of their seats and stampeded towards the windows.

"NO RUNNING!" commanded Ms. Hanks, as she calmly strolled towards them.

The entire class crammed together in a heap. Twenty-four noses pressed against the glass as forty-eight eyes eagerly searched the sky.

"Where? I don't see anything!" whined Natalie.

"Nothing unusual up there," noted Michael Peabody Smith III.

"LOOK!" exclaimed Billy, pointing.

Everyone traced the invisible line from Billy's finger up to the Sky. Slowly, a magnificent ribbon of pure light appeared as if strewn across the heavens above. It glistened in the sun like a fine thread of diamonds.

"Whoa, what kind of airplane leaves a trail like *that*?!" gasped Michael Peabody Smith III.

"That's no airplane, Michael," replied Ms. Hanks. "That's

your classmate, Jai."

"THAT'S JAI?!!!" exclaimed the class.

"Let's just say she's learned how to walk," grinned Ms. Hanks.

"All the way up there?" gasped Billy.

"Which leads us to our next topic: *Meteorology: the study of the earth's atmosphere.* Everyone, RETURN TO YOUR SEATS PLEASE."

"But—"

"Billy, thank you for pointing Jai out to us. You'll get your next assignment on her soon enough. Everyone, take out your science books."

"But—"

Billy, and the rest of the class for that matter, didn't understand Ms. Hanks *at all.* How could she just continue with class after that? What about Jai? How did she get up there? What WAS that thing she was walking on? Everyone pressed Ms. Hanks for answers, but she refused to address the topic any further.

"Everything in its proper time and place," was all she said.

At recess Billy and the rest of the class marveled at the luminous thread that still laced through the sky. The school principal walked by without noticing anything at all. When they asked about this after recess, Ms. Hanks simply answered, "Well, that's False Time for you."

"But what does that *mean*, 'False Time'?" asked Michael Peabody Smith III, frustrated.

"Just be glad you don't know what it is," replied Ms. Hanks, as if that was supposed to make sense.

"This is *torture!*" Billy murmured to himself. Even the Water Trees were mysterious about these latest developments. Whenever he asked them about Jai's whereabouts, all they'd say was, "Great Adventures simply take time to reveal themselves."

"Ugh!"

CHAPTER 16

Jai soon learned that walking over the world on a beam of light was easier than she had expected, more like skating. She glided swiftly across the planet with each step. It seemed like she had just begun but, when she double-checked her map, she realized she was already halfway there.

Pleased with her progress, a simple thought occurred to her: *I'm making such great time, I might as well stop for a minute and enjoy this amazing view. Who knows, I may never have a chance like this again!*

The beam of light was solid as a rock. She knew she could trust it. She sat down and marveled at the world before her.

Jai spotted the swirl of a typhoon far below. From such a height, it appeared calm and tranquil. Astonished, she realized that it was, in fact, the exact same shape—precisely the same swirl—she had seen in the seashells and land snails from her teacher's collection. "So THAT'S what Ms. Hanks meant about circles and patterns being present everywhere!"

Jai readjusted to a more comfortable position, casually swinging her legs over the edge of the light. As she settled herself in, she noticed an unusually dense cloud drifting towards her.

"Hello," muttered the cloud.

"Hi! How are you today?" returned Jai, delighted to be talking to a cloud.

"I've never seen a girl up here before," the cloud went on, completely ignoring her greeting. "Where are you headed?"

"To that island off in the ocean. Jai beamed, "I'm about halfway there!"

"You know, I've never heard of a human ever going there—or ever coming back for that matter. Are you sure that's a good idea? I don't think that's possible."

"Sure it's possible! The signs told me to go."

"Well, I wouldn't go if I were you," warned the cloud. "But good luck anyway... You'll need it."

"Uh, okay, thanks?" Jai said, as the cloud drifted away.

Soon, two more clouds passed by, smaller than the first, but as dense as thick gray cotton.

"Good morning!" chimed Jai.

"Hello." The clouds answered in unison.

"Beautiful day here, up in the Sky and all. Where are you guys headed?" Jai asked.

"Oh nowhere in particular," the clouds replied. "And yourself?"

"I'm headed for that island over there, you barely see it out from here."

"Oh that? You're just wasting your time," said the one cloud.

"But, that's what the signs have told me to do," Jai respectfully protested.

"Nothing important has ever come from visiting *that* place," said the other cloud. "Why don't you just hang here with us for a while?"

"Well, where are you guys going?" asked Jai.

The two clouds looked at one another. "We're just gonna drift. You know, we're clouds..."

"I'm pretty sure I should still at least go check it out," muttered Jai.

"Well, better you than me." said the one cloud.

"That's for sure," echoed the other. "Better you than me."

And with that, they drifted away.

Jai felt a heaviness in her heart. *I wonder what they're talking about? Is this a sign? I'm supposed to pay attention to signs.*

Soon, another cloud approached.

"Hello," said the cloud. "What brings you to this part of the world?"

"I'm on my way to that island over there. I, uh, guess."

"*THAT* island?" asked the cloud.

"Uh, yeah."

"That's clear on the other side of the world. There's no way you're ready for that! And anyway, *everyone* knows not to go there! Are you sure you know what you're doing?"

"I think so.

"You *think?*"

"The sign told me that I should... "

"Signs? Hmpf!" interrupted the cloud, "In all my time spanning the planet, I've never heard of anything so ridiculous!

A *sign* showing someone what to do! That's *crazy!*" With that said, it quietly drifted away.

Gradually, the entire sky filled with thick gray clouds, all warning her not to go to the island. Some said she wasn't smart enough, or old enough. Many asked her why she'd ever want to try anything so foolish.

Jai sat quietly as her enthusiasm slowly drained away. Like a clogged sink, all that was left in her mind was a dank puddle of doubt and concern. She felt incredibly alone.

What if there's something really terrible there? she brooded.

Looking out at the world below, an even worse thought occurred to her: *Maybe I wanted a Great Adventure SO bad that I saw signs that weren't really there.*

Suddenly, the beam of light from The Leather and The Sun began to shake.

Jai was terrified. "What's happening?!"

She grasped at the light, but her hands went right through it, as if it were vapor. She scrambled frantically for a split second, trying to hoist herself back up, but it was too late. She was falling. Flailing helplessly, her heart pounding in her ears, she plummeted towards the earth below.

Jai's body sliced through the Sky like a torpedo. Her hair and clothes flapped uncontrollably; the wind stretched her face and she could no longer feel her lips. The Leaf hunkered down in her back pocket.

"HEEEEEEEEEEELLLLLLLLLLLLLLLLLPPPPPPP!!!!!" Jai screamed as she dropped towards a dark gray blotch of land.

The fast-approaching forest grew larger and larger. Jai smashed into the first of the towering gray pine trees at breakneck speed. It felt like she didn't miss a branch as she drilled into the canopy, taking one painful body blow after another. The flexible pine limbs had begun to slow her descent, but not enough. Seconds later, worse than any belly flop, Jai smacked face down and unconscious into a mold-infested mattress of pine needles and rotting foliage.

CHAPTER 17

Billy woke up in a cold sweat. He'd had a nightmare—Jai was in some sort of dark forest, drowning in mud.

It was early morning. He sprang out of bed and ran downstairs. As usual, his parents were absorbed in reading their morning paper, so he easily crept past them and slipped out the front door, ignoring breakfast.

In a flash, he raced past the Grove and could have sworn he saw Jai's dad walking towards the Eldest Tree with a notebook in his hand. THAT was a shock, but there was no time to stop.

He bolted past the bus, the local train station, and all the way across town until he finally reached the school. His tennis shoes squeaked loudly as he jetted past kids in the hall and careened into his classroom. He almost ran into Ms. Hanks, who was calmly scribbling equations on the chalkboard.

"MS. HANKS! MS. HANKS!" Billy was panting.

His teacher turned around and her right eyebrow immediately shot up in alarm.

"What happened to *you*?"

It was only then that Billy noticed his t-shirt was on inside out AND backwards. The shirt tag was sticking out the front like a defiant tongue. He was also still wearing his Star Fighter pajama bottoms, and was missing his right sock.

"Your mother let you leave the house like that?"

"Uhhhhh, what? Sorry, I, uh, I was in a hurry."

"What's going on, Billy?"

"It's Jai. Something's wrong!"

"How do you know?"

"I had a bad dream. Like she's in some sort of very bad place. I don't really remember it, but I just know something's REALLY wrong. Ms. Hanks, you have to do something!"

"Hmmmm." She walked to the classroom windows and gazed up into the sky.

"Well, what do you know—"

"WHAT?" cried Billy, panicked.

Ms. Hanks turned to him.

"It'll be okay, Billy. Have a seat."

"But—"

"We'll get started after the bell rings. Don't worry. We'll handle this as a class."

At the bell, everyone poured into the room, making their way to their respective desks. Ms. Hanks stood before the class and announced, "Good morning, everyone. Quiet down please. Billy has apparently been informed that Jai is in need of some assistance."

All eyes turned to Billy. He nervously tugged at the tag protruding from the front of his shirt, his uncombed hair stuck out in all directions.

"What's wrong?" gulped Natalie.

"She'll be fine," answered Ms. Hanks calmly, "but she does need our help."

"What should we do?" asked Billy.

"It's simple," answered Ms. Hanks. "But we will all need to focus together."

"On what?" asked Michael Peabody Smith III, wiping the lenses of his thick, black-framed glasses with his shirt-tail.

"Now what did the Water Trees tell you the day Jai left?" she asked the class.

Silence. Conversations with adults about the Water Trees were almost unheard of.

"Come on, now," encouraged Ms. Hanks.

"Uh," stammered Billy, "The oldest Tree told us to see Jai as safe and well."

"Exactly! So that's what we must do. Now class, repeat after me: Home."

"Home?" asked Billy. "As in—*house*?!"

"*Home*," repeated Ms. Hanks firmly. "Simply repeat it and feel the sound of it, as you do so. We need to say it together and focus our thoughts entirely on Jai. It's easy if you put your mind to it. Just SEE Jai being safe and well."

"Why 'home'?" asked Michael Peabody III. As the Class Brain, he wondered how this worked scientifically.

"Michael, you have to say this one with your heart, not just your brain," answered Ms. Hanks. "Consider this a *higher* science."

He pushed his glasses up from his nose and tried to focus.

"Was Jai abducted by aliens?" asked Natalie Snoot,

frightened.

"Absolutely not! Let's just say that she didn't exactly follow instructions, and now she's in a bit of a bind."

"Yeah, that sounds like Jai," thought Billy.

"Now, everyone—close your eyes," instructed Ms. Hanks. "Let's all take a breath and repeat after me."

Except for the old clock ticking above the chalkboard, the room went silent.

"Home..."

"Home..."

"Home..."

Fifty-two eyes remained tightly shut and twenty-six mouths repeated "home" as Ms. Hanks and the class sent their good thoughts out to Jai, seeing her safe and well. Billy imagined her running fast and free. Natalie pictured her enjoying her stick of Perma-Lip. Each student, in their own way, envisioned Jai in a safe space. Ms. Hanks did the same.

After the ninth "home," Ms. Hanks abruptly announced, "Okay, class. Well done! Please open your eyes. It's time for math."

"Math?" protested Billy. "What about Jai?!"

"Nine 'homes' is sufficient." Ms. Hanks reached for her chalk.

"Sufficient for what?" demanded Billy.

"We all fall sometimes. And sometimes we simply need a jump start to get back up."

Everyone in class exchanged glances. No one had a clue what Ms. Hanks was talking about.

"Did that really help? Will she be okay?" asked Natalie, biting her lip.

"Absolutely. Now, everyone, get out your math lessons."

As the class reluctantly opened their books, Ms. Hanks glanced at Billy and gently smiled.

"Good work, Billy. You don't have to worry anymore. Trust me."

Billy simply nodded, relieved but still confused.

CHAPTER 18

Jai groaned. The word "home" rang in her ears like an incessant alarm clock, echoing and ricocheting inside her skull. Still dazed, she rolled slowly onto her side and reached to scratch her ear. Her eyes popped open as she touched something gooey on her face. Jerking her hand away, she looked at her fingers and cringed; they were dripping with dark, slimy goo.

Jai had no idea how long she'd been unconscious on this moldy pile of gray pine needles and rotting underbrush. Everything hurt. But she couldn't just lie there. Grimacing, she hoisted herself up and groped for her back pocket. At least the Leaf was still there. It immediately morphed into a redheaded woodpecker and flew to a nearby gray tree. Jai peered at her strange surroundings.

The big gray blotch she had fallen towards turned out to be some sort of swampy forest. Its dense canopy of trees obscured most of the light. Everything sagged. Hot and sticky, the dank air smelled like boiled sewage. Her skin began to itch.

Holding her nose, Jai turned her head upwards and squinted at the sky—or what little there was to find of it. Amidst an endless entanglement of branches, she spotted the beam of light from the Leather and the Sun. It had remained in place, still sparkling across the heavens.

UGH! Why did I have to stop? I should have just kept walking like I was told!

But it was too late. The thin strand of shimmering light was now impossibly far away. She thought of calling The Leather and The Sun back to her, but then remembered that the Mosquito had warned her not to do this before reaching the island.

The woodpecker, in the meantime, was happily pecking away at an enormous rotting tree. Jai noticed a sign leaning at its trunk, enveloped in weeds.

"A sign!" Jai exclaimed in relief.

Stepping towards it, her foot slipped into a rut of heavy brownish sludge. The mud belched rudely as she tugged her shoe from its grip. To make matters worse, she realized that she was completely surrounded by the brackish goop. She'd have to trudge directly through it in order to get anywhere. With great hesitation, she slid her foot into the gunk.

"Ugh!"

Gray-brown slime slowly oozed into her socks and between her toes. The mud glugged and belched, releasing clouds of putrid vapor with each step. Jai slogged her way to the sign, her face slightly purple from gagging. Meanwhile, the woodpecker continued pecking happily away. Her shoes and lower pant legs now thoroughly soaked in disgusting glop, Jai cleared the sign of its weeds and read the bad news:

She glanced at the woodpecker.

"I'm lost."

The bird nodded in agreement as it wrestled a juicy, struggling, brown grub out of a hole and downed it with a single gulp. Satisfied, it morphed back into a Leaf and floated to the ground map-side-up.

An ominous dark blotch now appeared on the map, exactly half way between The Top of the World and the island.

Jai took a breath to center herself, a dangerous thing to do when everything stinks *that* bad, but she had to try. Just then, a thought popped into her brain. The Eldest Tree had told her what to do if she got lost.

"If you ever think you've taken a wrong turn, all you need to do is roll the Leaf up like a telescope and look through it. It will show you how to get back to where you were before you got off track."

She quickly rolled the Leaf up into a scroll and peered through it.

As if watching a movie through a telescope, Jai saw herself being carried up in into the sky by an enormous eagle. The magnificent bird held her securely by its talons, clutching the back of her shirt. With lightning speed, the eagle soared through the heavens, with Jai in tow. Soon, they reached the beam of light from the Leather and The Sun where she was safely dropped off.

Jai lowered the Leaf from her eye.

Well, that's easy! she thought, her mood brightening.

Jai smiled at the Leaf and announced: "Okay, I'm ready! You can turn into an eagle now and take me back. Let's get out of here!"

The Leaf sat in her hands, motionless. It didn't morph into anything.

Jai decided to change her approach:

"Um, would you *PLEASE* turn into an eagle now and take me back?"

Nothing. It wouldn't budge.

She glanced at the trees that drooped all around her and noticed another sign. It read:

THE LARGE GRAY BUIDLING WILL HELP YOU FIND SOME VERY MUCH NEEDED PEACE OF MIND.

Desperate for clues, she re-inspected the map and discovered that a particularly large building had appeared. It sat on the outskirts of the blotch.

"Okay," thought Jai, *"One way or another, I'm going to find that place. I really mean it."*

There were no paths in *The Land of the Lost*. Water Tree

Maps are always accurate; the area was nothing but a blotch—crammed with dense moldy foliage. Not knowing what else to do, she trudged headfirst into the bleak terrain.

Jai could see no further than three feet ahead. With each step she had to pull away a gnarly branch or untangle her foot from a thorny bush. At one point, she wondered if she was actually going in circles. She was about to turn around when she detected the smell of smoke. Jai pushed through the maze, until there, in a clearing, she saw an old man warming his hands by a fire. The clammy air held the smoke in place—creating a dense haze. Jai trotted up to him in relief.

"Hi!"

The old man slowly looked up from the fire.

"Well, I'll be! A girl!"

His clothes were faded and ragged, his skin as gray as the trees.

Jai smiled at the old man, still feeling hopeful.

"I'm looking for a big gray building. Have you seen it?"

"Hmmmm, in all the years I've been here, I don't think I've ever heard of such a thing."

"How long *have* you been here?"

"Oh, about as long as I can remember. Now, what's a nice girl like you doing out here?"

"Well, I fell out of the sky recently."

"Oh, that was you?"

"Yeah."

"I heard you on your way down. Good set of lungs there, kid."

"Thanks."

Jai looked at the man. He was the oldest looking person she'd ever seen, yet his smile was soft and gentle.

"Why, back when I was your age. I always dreamed about flying through the sky in a contraption I called an air-buggy."

"You mean, like an airplane?"

"An ear-what?"

Jai paused. She thought he was kidding. How could anyone not know about airplanes?

"An AIR-plane. You know, it's something you fly in to get from one place to another."

The man's smile hardened as a cloud of pessimism crossed over his lips.

"Ridiculous! There's no such thing!"

Jai stood dumbfounded before the old man.

"How long did you say you've been here?"

"Too long to remember."

"You know, they've invented airplanes."

"Right," replied the old man sarcastically. "You have a good imagination kid, but we both know that's a bunch of hogwash."

"But Mr..."

"You know, people were right. I remember as a boy, whenever I'd draw pictures of my flying machine, everyone insisted it could never be done. It was one of the last things I remember hearing before I somehow ended up here."

What kind of place is this? she thought. A shiver raced down her spine.

"Why don't you run along now and play, kid?" said the

man, motioning for her to leave.

The old man looked so lonely and miserable, Jai wanted to cry. She wondered if he'd ever had a friend. She thought of her dad. Her heart drooped a little more. She hoped he would never feel that alone.

"You heard me, run along."

Not knowing what else to do, she walked up to him and gently kissed his cheek. His whiskers were hard as tacks.

"Would you like to come with me?"

"Naw. Just run along now."

The old man remained silent, slowly tending the fire, and Jai turned to leave. She didn't see it, but his eyes were filled with tears.

Jai quickly discovered that the Land of the Lost was anything but deserted. Each person she met was completely alone and convinced they were the only ones there. They spoke to her of discarded hopes and crushed dreams. Some rambled on about their failures. Others were angry and bitter. Most were sad or insecure. A few were arrogant. But one thing was for certain: everyone was miserable. Worst of all, none of them had ever heard of the mysterious gray building, and none of them were particularly interested in it either.

Jai stumbled upon a large stagnant pond. Thick clouds of gnats swarmed along the surface, feasting on clumps of floating bacteria. At the opposite bank knelt an extraordinarily beautiful woman who was staring into the murky water.

Jai skirted the pond and approached the woman. She seemed to be inspecting her face in the reflection of the pond's surface—repeatedly adjusting her hair while turning her head from side to side, mumbling to herself.

"I'm so ugly. Just look at me! I'm hideous!"

"You're not ugly!" replied Jai. "You're really pretty!"

The beautiful woman didn't hear her. She continued staring at her reflection in disgust.

"Why are you doing that?" exclaimed Jai. "Let's get out of here!"

A swirl of gnats was now hovering nearby.

"Look," continued Jai, shooing away the edge of the swarm, "there's a building somewhere around here that can help. Let's find it!"

As the beautiful woman rambled on to herself about how ugly she was, a gnat zoomed straight up Jai's nose. Her head was now under direct attack—gnats darted towards her eyes and into her ears. Flailing wildly, Jai dashed away from the pond, away from the gnats, and away from the beautiful woman who hadn't looked up even once.

Being in the Land of the Lost reminded Jai of the time when Dax Googan, the school bully, glued a boy to his seat in class. Dax had squeezed an entire bottle of Superglue onto the boy's chair while he was in the bathroom. When the boy returned and sat down, his pants and bottom instantly bonded to the chair. The janitor and school nurse had to team up with turpentine and Q-tips for over an hour before separating his backside from the chair. His mom had to bring him a second pair of pants and the entire class waited in the hall while he changed.

To Jai, it seemed like everyone she met was just glued

there, hopelessly stuck. *The Land of the Lost* was the bleakest, most dreadful place she'd ever been. In Great Adventure terms, on a one-to-ten scale, she concluded that it ranked a whopping minus five, rivaled only by her annual visits to the dentist—and even *those* rated a minus one.

As she plodded on, Jai lost all track of time. Eventually, she spotted a cluster of small, colored lights blinking in the distance. As she made her way towards them, she found a man sitting alone on a decaying log, staring into an unusual contraption that looked like some sort of floating computer. The sleek screen emitted an oddly pleasing, yellow light. Several buttons lined its frame, blinking in a variety of colors. Most intriguing to Jai was the miniature airplane propeller at the top of the machine. The blades whirled jubilantly without making the slightest noise, as the entire contraption hovered in mid-air.

The man sat engrossed before the screen, busily pushing buttons. He was immaculately dressed in a crisp business suite, sleek leather shoes and a most impressive diamond watch. With every flick of his wrist, it sparkled brilliantly against the dreary foliage. This man was possibly the wealthiest person she'd ever seen—an odd sight amongst all the decay.

"Hi," offered Jai.

"Hello," answered the man, not looking away from his screen.

"What is that thing?"

The man's lips curled into a grin.

"This 'THING' is my dream machine. A Mind Master 3000. The ultimate in floating communications systems."

Jai looked curiously at the monitor.

"What's it do?"

The man stared into the screen, his eyes shining in the glow.

"WHY, ONLY EVERYTHING! The entire world is right here at my fingertips. I can watch *anything* while I make my billions!"

"You mean, it's like a TV?"

"Far more advanced," boasted the man. "The Mind Master 3000 has over 700,000 channels. It can send and retrieve information about *anything* from *anywhere* in less than a nanosecond. It's indispensable for building my business empire. With my Mind Master I can hire and fire anyone in the world in an instant! Do anything I want! All with the simple push of a button! My profits are SOARING! And it even makes a good cup of coffee."

Jai peered curiously at the mysterious floating device while the man continued fidgeting with the controls.

"This is the *ultimate* in intelligence. But it's not for everyone. It's like a very exclusive club—only a few of us have one."

"Wow!' exclaimed Jai. "Who'd ever think that something like that would end up in *The Land of the Lost*!"

"The Land of the what?"

"You know, *The Land of the Lost*, where we are right now."

"I don't know what you're talking about. I've never heard of such a place."

Jai peered curiously at the man. "Um—I'm looking for a gray building that's around here somewhere. Could your Mind

Master help me find it?"

The man, absorbed in pushing buttons, ignored her completely.

There wasn't much else to say. Shrugging, she turned to leave but then stopped in her tracks. She thought she heard someone humming. Glancing up, she noticed a fresh green Stem protruding from a branch just above her head. It sported an enormous pair of wire-rimmed glasses and was humming happily to itself, reading a book.

"A Stem!" squealed Jai in delight

"Of course. Not *everyone* here is lost, you know." The Stem glanced down distastefully at the businessman engrossed in his screen. "Then again, most are."

The man didn't notice.

"What are you reading?" asked Jai.

"Ah, an all-time forest favorite: *Great Stems and The Branches They Grow On*. Literature at its best."

"I don't think I've read it."

"Hey, will you be quiet?" snapped the man. His eyes narrowed to crinkled slits as he stared in the screen. "You're distracting me! Can't you see I'm busy?"

"Even too busy to help a kid who's lost?" scorned the Stem.

The man flicked his hand, as if shooing away a fly.

"Hey, I'm in the middle of reviewing my latest profit report. This is important."

"Your contraption is fully equipped to locate that gray building for her. She's only asking for some simple directions."

The man smirked, uninterested.

"Then let someone else do it. I'm busy."

"Hmmm. Selfish and LOST!" concluded the Stem. "It's bad enough that you're wasting a perfectly good idea, but this is unacceptable. You're even less intelligent than I thought!"

"I'm *intelligent*," scoffed the man. "I'm the smartest guy around! Just look at this!" The man pushed a few more buttons. Instantly, the screen displayed a long list of bank accounts, flaunting colossal amounts of money stashed in each. Jai looked into the monitor. Not ever, in any math class, had she ever seen numbers that huge.

The Stem crumpled its tiny nose in disgust. "And what are you going to *do* with all those profits? That's more money than one person, or even several people, could ever use in a lifetime!"

The man sneered, flicking a speck of mold off his suit.

"Why, keep it for myself of course! After all, that's the *intelligent* thing to do!"

"Hmmmm. We *Stems* have the definitive way of measuring intelligence—*the Royal Academy Final Exam*. All Stems everywhere must pass it in order to graduate. Want to find out how intelligent you *really* are? Take it, if you dare!"

"I can ace any test in the marketplace!" sneered the man. "I'll even bet my Mind Master on it! So what do I get when I win? I ALWAYS win."

The Stem inspected the man and coolly replied, "*If*—not _when_—you win, you'd get a second Mind Master 3000."

Jai wondered how a Stem could promise such a thing. The man, however, didn't question it in the least. The idea of doubling his earnings was too good to pass up.

"It's a deal!"

For the first time, he looked away from his monitor and realized that he had, in fact, just placed a bet with a Stem. He sat on his rotting log, thinking, *"I can't believe I'm actually talking to a stick."*

"My dear boy," noted the Stem, hearing the man's thought. "I'm a *Stem*. Are you not intelligent enough to see that?"

The man glared back. "Make it quick. My time's valuable. You should be glad I'm not charging you for this."

Jai's jaw dropped. "That's a *Stem* you're talking to!"

"Hmmf!" exclaimed the Stem. It proceeded to retrieve a small scroll of bark, unrolled it carefully, and read the opening contents aloud with great formality:

"Announcing: *'The Royal Academy Final Exam: The Definitive Test of Intelligence'*."

The man murmured, *"This'll be a piece of cake!"*

And then, to Jai's surprise, the Stem tossed her the miniature scroll.

"Go ahead, Honey," instructed the Stem. "Give the exam!"

"WHAT?" exclaimed Jai.

"I'm supposed to take an intelligence test from a child?!" protested the man, now furious.

"I'm not a child, I'm TEN!"

"Exactly!" exclaimed the man.

The Stem calmly glanced up at the Sky and said, "Music please."

On cue, the dreary forest was mysteriously filled with TV game show tick-tock music.

"Go for it, Honey," instructed the Stem to Jai.

"What do I do?"

"Simple. Just read the questions, one after the other."

Jai squinted at the scroll, cleared her throat, and read the first microscopic line. "Question Number One: When was the last time you noticed a flower blooming?"

"What does *that* have to do with anything? I don't sell flowers!" exclaimed the man.

The music was abruptly interrupted by a jarring, wrong-answer "BEEEEEEEEEEP!"

The game show music resumed, and Jai continued.

"Question Number Two: When was the last time you were kind to a stranger? Especially someone who really needed help?"

"BEEEEEEEEEEP!"

"Well, we already know the answer to *THAT* one, now don't we?" scorned the Stem sharply. Turning to Jai, the Stem nodded and the music played on.

"Question Number Three: When was the last time you expressed gratitude?"

"Uh—"

"Or stopped to watch a sunset?"

"What?"

"Or *really* listened to what someone else was saying?"

"Hey, people listen to ME! It's in *that* order."

"Or thanked the planet you're living on for sustaining you?"

"Are you kidding?"

"Or asked yourself why you're even here to begin with?"

"Huh?"

BEEEEEEEEEEEEEEP!

"My dear man," concluded the Stem, "this marks the end of your exam! It wasn't too hard to predict this, but I'll make it official: you FLUNK!"

And with that, the Mind Master's propeller spurted a weak cough and blipped off completely. The lifeless monitor plunged to the ground, landing on a heap of putrid debris.

Clenching his fists, the man stared in disbelief at the lifeless, mud-splattered screen. All was silent, except for his rotting log, which creaked a little.

"Of course," added the Stem after a while, "you get a bonus question if you like. You might as well try to redeem yourself."

"What have you got to lose?" added Jai. After all, flunking was the worst. She tossed the scroll back to the Stem.

"I'll even read the question to you myself," noted the Stem with great pride.

"Well, WHAT IS IT?!" The man's eyes were now bulging with anger. "Get on with it!"

Amused, the Stem continued with great dramatic flair, "When was the last time you smelled the roses?"

The man smirked, "What roses?"

"ANY roses!"

"Uh... she already asked me about flowers," whined the man. Then, suddenly, his face brightened. He even smiled—revealing a row of yellow teeth. "Hey, now I get it! Is this really some sort of investment opportunity? A chance to buy up all flower seeds—everywhere? Why stop there? Why not buy up all seeds everywhere? I'll own it all! What a great idea!"

"BEEEEEEEEEEEEEEEEEEEEP!"

"Congratulations!" exclaimed the Stem, "You have managed to earn the lowest score in history! You, my boy, are DONE! No more Mind Master for you!"

The man scowled in fury.

The Stem continued. "Throughout the ages and even now, roses continue to offer their beauty—free of charge—for *everyone* to enjoy, no matter who they are." Glancing down at the man, it added, "Here's an intelligent question for you to ask yourself: Why did that Mind Blaster contraption come to you in the first place? It's not what you think!"

"*Mind Master*," corrected the man. "And what do you mean?" He looked genuinely confused.

"You had a good idea once." The Stem now spoke with the precision and insight of a true *Royal Academy* graduate. "You were always meant to be successful. But not like this. And if you go with her to that grey building she was asking you about, you'll find out what I mean."

The man glanced at the endless maze of rotting foliage all around. He hadn't noticed any of it before. Overwhelmed, he mumbled, "I'd get lost."

The Stem sighed, rolling its eyes. "You ARE lost!"

There in the clammy silence, the man felt horribly alone. Eventually he spoke.

"I need some time to think."

"Now THAT would be different!" replied the Stem.

Just then, the Leaf fell from Jai's pocket, morphed into a bright yellow finch, and darted away.

"Time to go!" announced Jai. She turned to the man. "So, you wanna come with me?"

Unable to look at her, the man stared at his hands and shook his head, "No."

"He may leave here one day," said the Stem, "but not today."

And with that, the Stem placed an enormous pair of reading glasses on its nose, and chose another classic from its tiny bookcase: *The Royal Album of Stemology: Spring Edition.*

Not knowing what else to say, Jai waved to the man and offered, "Good luck!"

"Thanks. You too." Somehow, his voice had softened a bit.

"And thanks!" she continued, nodding respectfully to the Stem. "Thank you for everything!"

"You're welcome, Jai." The Stem opened its book and swayed gently, humming happily to itself.

Jai waded back into the brush.

"And one more thing," called out the Stem. "You're only ninety-seven point three paces away."

"You mean, from the building?" asked Jai, turning around.

"Indeed," replied the Stem. "It's a bit of a climb, but you'll get there."

"Alright! Which way should I go?"

"Just follow your Leaf."

"Thanks!"

And with that, she lumbered on. Soon after, the man

peered up into the sky amidst the quagmire of tangled branches.

"What's *that*?" he asked the Stem, marveling at a brilliant thread of light that sparkled across the heavens.

CHAPTER 19

Ninety-seven point three paces sounded easy enough. Jai stumbled on. But the ground below her was completely rotten, making it almost impossible to get anywhere. She sank deep into the spongy glop—all the way up to her knees. To make matters worse, the entire forest now rose on an incline. She grabbed onto crumbling branches as she climbed, sometimes slipping and skidding backwards, but gradually making headway. Meanwhile, the yellow finch chirped and darted from tree to tree, gleefully leading the way. After pushing past a particularly dense wall of vines, she at last stepped onto an open plateau of green grass. She ran a few steps and dropped to the ground, rolling ecstatic summersaults on the soft, lush grass. She'd made it!

She had been in the shadows of the Land of the Lost for so long, it took a moment for her eyes to adjust to the sun. Shielding her brow with her hand, she squinted at the well-manicured lawn that sprawled before her. A very long sidewalk ran down its center. At the end of the walkway, an enormous gray cement building shot up from the ground. Above the double door entrance, chiseled in majestic bold letters, was written: **THE BUREAU OF LOST IDEAS**.

Jai heaved a sigh of relief and wiped the remaining grime from her hands onto her pants. Even though she was out of *The Land of the Lost*, its stench was still on her clothing. The slimy fabric stuck to her skin. Her shoes and socks were soaked in rancid gunk. Trying not to think about it, she headed towards the building. Meanwhile, the finch landed on her shoulder and began to sing as they arrived at the entrance.

"Shhhhh!"

The finch nodded and fell silent.

Jai pushed hard against the enormous door. It made a long, eerie squeal as it creaked open.

She peered in. The building seemed to be deserted. As she inched her way past its threshold, the door slammed heavily behind her. Looking around, she gasped. Towering stone walls rose high above with only a few windows at the top. The air was stale. The whole place felt like some kind of dungeon or tomb. Amidst the shadows, enormous piles of paper shot up like pillars, draped in heavy cobwebs.

"This must be the wrong building."

She turned and pulled at the door, but it wouldn't open. She yanked at it again. Not so much as a budge. She was locked in. At that moment, she heard slow ominous footsteps coming from the shadows at the back of the room.

clomp...clomp...clomp....

Her throat ran dry. The only other time she'd heard steps like that was in a horror movie she and Billy had watched one time when her dad was at work. Her heart raced as she tugged frantically at the door. The steps were getting closer.

Clomp...clomp...clomp...

The hair stood up on the back of Jai's neck. She tried again. The door still wouldn't budge. The footsteps grew even closer.

Desperate, Jai released the doorknob and ran.

Clomp...clomp...clomp...

The steps quickened.

She zigzagged through a maze of towering stacks, and abruptly stopped. Like a fly caught in a spider's web, there was nowhere to go. Nowhere to run. Jai was trapped.

Clomp...

The footsteps stopped directly behind her. Jai tried to scream, but no sound came out. Clenching her arms and trembling, she suddenly heard...

"Achoo!"

A sneeze? Jai thought as she turned around, stunned. Just then a friendly-looking old woman stepped out of the shadows.

"Bless you," offered Jai. Her voice cracked slightly.

"Why, thank you!" replied the old woman, retrieving a tissue from her pocket.

Her lean wiry frame was crowned with a thick mop of white hair that bounced as she walked. She wore a white cotton shirt with rolled up sleeves, gray baggy pants and a bleached white apron with the word "**ZING!**" emblazoned across the front. Her eyes conveyed a bright, clear light from behind immensely thick bifocals. Jai smiled. The frames were the very shade of blue that she loved so much.

"How wonderful!" continued the old woman. "Someone has finally come to retrieve an idea! Welcome!"

"Uh—thanks."

"You know, I've been meaning to get that door fixed! Anyway, my name is Grelda."

"Hi Grelda. My name's Jai. Uh, what *is* this place?"

"Why, didn't you see the sign outside? This is the official Bureau of Lost Ideas. Every time anyone, anywhere, has a good idea, neglects it, or gives up on it for whatever reason, the idea is written up into a report and brought here in the hopes that they, or someone else, will come back for it someday."

"So this is kind of like a 'lost and found'?"

"Precisely."

Grelda walked over to a nearby wall and flipped on the light. Jai soon discovered that the Bureau was more like a colossal warehouse than a dungeon. The entire building was filled with towering stacks of paper and walls of file cabinets. And *everything* was covered in dust.

"When's the last time anyone came here?" asked Jai, looking around at all the dust.

"Long time. You see that pile over there?" Grelda pointed to a mountain of paper stacked precariously to the ceiling.

"Yeah."

"Well, those are all reports of great inventions that were never made. And do you know why they were never made?"

"No."

"Because the people who had all of those great and wonderful ideas lost them. So they ended up here instead."

"How did they lose their ideas to begin with?" asked Jai.

"Well, let's put it this way: How did YOU get here?"

"Me? Well, I fell out of the Sky."

"I see." The woman looked deeply at Jai.

"Uh, I'm on a Great Adventure." Jai continued, "Do you have a report for me too?"

"Probably. I just got something in today about a girl with a Water Tree Leaf."

"That's me."

"Thought so."

"So what does the report say?" Jai asked.

"Well, hang on just a minute. I have to find it."

Grelda walked over to a file cabinet labeled "New Arrivals." Jai couldn't help but notice that she moved with remarkable agility.

Reading her thoughts, Grelda replied, "Never believe what they tell you about aging, kid! And, by the way, *I'm* not lost!"

The woman flashed such an exuberant and youthful smile—so filled with joy—that Jai laughed out loud.

"Now, let's see." The old woman rummaged through her file folders. "There's 'Great Books Never Written,' 'Great Songs Never Sung,' 'Kind Actions Never Taken,' 'Beautiful Friendships Never Made.' Ah, here we go: 'Wonderful Places Never Gone To.'"

The old woman took out a sheet of paper and read it carefully. "Hmmm. It says here you were given the idea to go to a magical island."

"Yeah, just like the signs said," muttered Jai.

"Hmmmm, says here that you 'fell off the light.'"

"Yeah, that's me."

"That's a pretty serious thing, you know." Grelda, glanced up from her bifocals.

"I feel awful about it," confided Jai.

"Well, let's see what else it says here."

Jai glanced around at the piles of paper as the old woman continued reviewing the report.

"Ah, yes, it says here that you have suffered a hearing problem."

"A hearing problem?"

"Yes, indeed. You've been listening to the crowd instead of yourself."

"Well, I *did* talk to some clouds when I sat down. Maybe it's a misprint. I talked to a cloud, not a crowd."

"No, these reports are always accurate. It says here that you let those dark clouds discourage you, and that you need to have your ears cleaned."

"My ears cleaned? Does that hurt?"

"No, not at all. But first, before we do anything else, it's company policy to check your conviction level."

Grelda reached under her desk and retrieved a small machine with the words, "Conviction Meter" printed across the front. It consisted of a square metal box with a red dial at the top. A bright orange tube protruded from one side and a small purple ball dangled on the end of the tube. The gadget softly whirred as Grelda sat it on the desk.

"Have you ever had your conviction measured before?"

"Uh, no. I don't really know what 'conviction' is."

"Conviction, my Dear, is something very special that you

are born with. It is the power of belief in yourself and in all of the good ideas that come to you."

"Oh, you mean, like when I know I can do anything, no matter what?"

"Exactly." The woman handed the purple ball to Jai. "Here, you need to hold this for thirty seconds for the test to be accurate."

Jai did as the old woman instructed. A half-minute later, the machine beeped.

"Okay, you're all done." Grelda carefully studied the dial on the machine.

"Yes, just as I suspected. Your conviction level is pretty low right now. That always happens you know, when a person listens to the wrong voices."

"What do I do?" asked Jai, worried.

"Well, let's take a look here." Grelda peered into one of Jai's ears.

"Hmmmm. Seems you've been hearing a lot of fearful thoughts lately."

"How can you tell?" asked Jai.

"Well, they're still in your ears."

"Really?"

"Yes, indeed. I can see them right in there." The woman inspected Jai's other ear.

"Are you talking about all that stuff those clouds said about the island?" Jai asked.

"Exactly. You see, deep in your heart you knew that going to the island was the right thing to do, but when all those clouds insisted that you were wrong, you started to doubt what you knew. That's how you got lost. That's when you fell off the light."

"Because I heard what those clouds were saying?"

"No, because you *listened to* what those clouds were saying. There's a big difference."

"Oh."

"You took their word for it without ever questioning if what they were saying was correct."

"But, how could I tell?"

"Ah, that's simple." Grelda pointed to a poster on the wall behind her desk. It read:

How to Lose a Good Idea the Easy Way—
Two Discouraging Phrases

*** What, are you CRAZY?! **You can't do *that*!** ***
*** "Aww, c'mon, you can **do it tomorrow**." ***

If you encounter either of these,
please contact the Bureau of Lost Ideas immediately.

"Every good idea in this room ended up here because someone took at least one of those phrases to heart.

"That first one sounds a lot like those clouds," Jai admitted.

"That's exactly right. You need to recognize this sort of thing for what it is and choose not to believe it. Be sure to watch out for the word 'can't,' Jai. And as for the second phrase, well, just don't put things off. Now come with me. I want to show you something."

Grelda strolled to the back of the building with Jai following close behind. She had never seen so many stacks of paper in her life. Each pile had a different category: 'Great Discoveries Never Found'; 'Beautiful Artwork Never Completed'; 'Apologies Never Made'; and even one pile that was labeled: 'Great Adventures Never Taken'. Jai gasped at the thought.

"Remain steadfast, Jai." The old woman continued walking.

"What does that mean?"

"It means you have to stay focused and determined and not let fear get to you—like it got to all these other people."

"How do I do that?"

"You'll see."

Walking amidst millions of lost ideas, Jai wondered about what had happened to all of the people who once had them. She guessed that she had met some of them in *The Land of the Lost.* She thought about the businessman and wondered if he was still sitting on that rotten log.

"Oh him?" answered Grelda, reading her thoughts. "He had a really great idea, but forgot all about it."

"So which of these ideas is his?"

"Well, I can't tell you that. Strict confidentiality is company policy around here." Grelda turned down an aisle and Jai quickened her pace to keep up. "But one thing's for sure: he's supposed to do something the world has never seen before.

Something remarkable that could help virtually everyone everywhere. And he was even given the technology to do it!"

"His idea must be the most important of all!"

"No, Dear," smiled the old woman, glancing back at her. "All dreams, all ideas are equally magnificent, no matter how big or how small. It's just like *The Rule Book* says on page seven."

Silence.

"Uh... I only read the first couple of pages."

"Well, that's no real surprise, Dear. If you knew all the rules, you definitely wouldn't have ended up here! On page seven it clearly states: 'Each idea is suited perfectly for the person it's given to, and everyone gets *at least* a few great ideas during their lifetime, but usually more than that.'"

"Everyone?"

"Absolutely! Every person everywhere, no matter what." Grelda made a quick left turn.

"Wow."

"And unlike what many people think, no one's ever too old to get a great idea. There'd be a lot less paper around here if people understood that."

Jai thought about her dad and wondered if any of these lost ideas belonged to him.

"Yes, a couple of them do," answered Grelda, reading her thought. She made a sharp right turn and waved for Jai to follow. They soon stood before a small tiled booth covered by a curtain. Grelda handed Jai a towel and a cloth bag.

"What's this?"

"Time for a shower." Nodding towards the booth, Grelda

added, "there's plenty of soap. Don't worry if you use it all. You may have to."

Jai looked into the bag. Remarkably, it contained a duplicate set of clothes—the exact ones Jai was wearing—only clean! It even included a fresh pair of shoes and socks.

Grelda winked at Jai with a twinkle in her eye.

"Courtesy of the Water Trees."

"But...how?"

The old woman just laughed with bravado. "Now, go wash up and we'll get those ears cleaned!"

Having gone so many days unbathed, Jai's shower felt miraculous. Three bars of soap later, she emerged refreshed and in clean, dry clothes. The finch swooped quickly to her shoulder, nodded approvingly and morphed back into a Leaf. She tucked it in her back pocket.

"What do I do with these?" asked Jai. Her stiff arm held out the bag containing her dirty clothes. It sagged heavily from all the grime and smelled like hot sewage.

"Did you take everything from the pockets?" asked Grelda, stepping back and holding her nose.

"Yeah."

"Good. I'll take care of those, just leave the bag over there and come with me."

She led Jai past several towering piles of paper, eventually arriving at a large overstuffed lounge chair. A massive, shiny-red vacuum cleaner with the words "Thought-O-Vac" emblazoned across the front sat next to it. Other than the shower stall, it was the only thing in the entire building that wasn't caked in dust.

"So, you've never had your ears cleaned before?" asked Grelda.

"Not with something like that." Jai cautiously eyed the vacuum. "Are you sure this won't hurt?"

"Promise. If anything, you'll feel much better after all those fearful thoughts are cleaned out."

"Well..." Jai paused. "Okay."

"Good. Now just have a seat and I'll get everything ready."

She plugged the vacuum cleaner into a nearby wall socket and flipped it on. Jai noticed a large, bright orange suction cup at the end of the nozzle.

"Now," Grelda spoke over the drone of the vacuum cleaner, "I'm going to put this suction cup over each of your ears, one at a time. It'll suck out all those bad thoughts."

"What if it sucks out the good ones too?" asked Jai, frightened.

"It can't do that. It'll only take out the ones that didn't belong there in the first place. Ready?"

"Well, OK, I guess so." Jai swung her feet nervously.

"Now, try to hold still."

As Grelda put the suction cup to her right ear, Jai was shocked to hear the clouds' voices all over again, only sped up.

"It's too far!"

"You're too young!"

"It's too dangerous!"

She could actually feel the voices leaving her head.

"This is amazing," shouted Jai over the vacuum cleaner.

"Works every time. Okay, that ear's done. Ready for the next one?"

"Ready!"

Grelda gently placed the suction cup over Jai's left ear.

"Wow, I had no idea that those voices were still in there! It's like they've been talking inside my head this whole time!"

"Exactly. That's why you have to be mindful of what you let in there. Grelda turned off the vacuum cleaner. "That's what being steadfast is all about."

"Wow, I feel so much better! Can I get my other ideas back now?"

"Well, how do you feel about going to the island?"

"I really want to!"

"What about those clouds?"

"Oh, they don't matter. They were just afraid. All their talk was about *them*, not me."

At that moment, a loud gong rang throughout the entire building.

"What was *that*?"

"That means you've just graduated. In other words, you're not listening to fearful thoughts anymore, so you're free to trust again. You can now have your ideas back."

"YES!" Jai shouted with a fist pump.

"All that's left at this point is for you to sign this release form. After that, you're all set."

"Release form?"

"It's company policy."

"Oh."

Grelda scribbled on a sheet of paper and handed it to Jai.

The top of the form featured the official Bureau logo: a drawing of the "Thought-O-Vac" sitting next to a "Conviction Meter." Below it, read the caption:

"Only *You* Can Prevent Lost Ideas.
Guard Your Ears!!!"

Under "Daily Maintenance," Grelda added: "Remember: You can do anything! Listen to the signs, not the cloud crowd."

Jai read the note carefully and scrawled her name on the dotted line at the bottom of the page.

"Thanks, Grelda!"

"My pleasure, Jai."

They walked together through the maze of piles, back to the front door.

"Stand back a minute, Jai."

Grelda ran straight for the door, rammed into it like a linebacker, and pulled the handle towards her. It opened with a shrill squeak. Jai stared at the old woman, wide-eyed. She couldn't get that door open no matter how hard she tried, and she was a zillion years younger. She didn't think older people could be that strong.

"We can do anything we set our minds to," replied Grelda, reading her thoughts. "When your mind is like a mirror, anything's possible! Just don't use it like a camera."

Hmmmm. One of the secrets of the Universe, thought Jai. She was just as confused hearing it the second time around.

The old woman smiled, her eyes sparkled especially bright.

"You'll find out soon enough."

Just then, the Leaf fell from Jai's back pocket and morphed into a brilliant red cardinal, the exact same color as the "Thought-O-Vac."

"Ya know," mused Jai as she watched the cardinal, "I met all sorts of people in *The Land of the Lost* who don't even know about this place. Maybe that's why nobody comes here."

"That's very possible." Grelda adjusted her glasses.

"There must be some way to let them know about it."

"Well, years ago, The Bureau printed a batch of flyers with directions."

"Do you still have them?"

"They're in the back."

"Can I see them?"

"Sure. Hang on." Grelda disappeared behind the piles and soon reemerged with a rusted shopping cart filled with dull-yellow flyers.

"These were colorful way-back-when," noted Grelda as she handed Jai a flyer.

Jai nodded and read carefully.

Retrieve your dreams at

THE BUREAU OF LOST IDEAS

Just 1 block south of *The Land of the Lost.*

No reservations necessary.

Open 24 hours.

Free toaster for the first 1000 customers.

"Free toaster?" asked Jai, looking up from the flyer.

"Just a little incentive to make the trip over here," replied Grelda.

"Oh."

In addition, an elaborate map was included at the bottom of the page. It showed how to get to The Bureau from anywhere in the world, even through the tangled mess of *The Land of the Lost.* Jai wished she'd seen one of these flyers sooner.

"Do you mind if I take all these?"

"No, not at all."

Jai grinned with a mischievous glint in her eyes.

"I have an idea."

"Good!" Grelda's white hair bounced around her face as she nodded enthusiastically.

"This is one idea that won't end up back in one of your piles," assured Jai. "Thanks for everything!"

"You're very welcome!" said Grelda. "Just leave the cart outside the front door when you're done. Oh, and Good luck!" Her eyes sparkled with zest as she waved goodbye.

Jai rolled the shopping cart past the door, and the cardinal darted after her. The rusty wheels squeaked on the pavement as she made her way down to the end of the sidewalk. Seeing the outer rim of *The Land of the Lost,* Jai shuddered. The thick gray forest—with its sagging trees and tangled vines—loomed heavily like a prison wall.

Happy to look elsewhere, she gazed up at the Sky. It seemed like it'd been forever since she last spoke to it. Clearing her throat, she decided to give it a try.

"Um...excuse me—I know it's been a while since I've talked to you, but would you please help me out?"

Silence.

Jai decided to wait and not ask again. After a long while, an enormous voice answered: "Yes, may I help you?"

"Do you know anything about distributing flyers?" asked Jai, gazing up into the heavens.

"Yes, I know a thing or two about it," boomed the infinite expanse.

"Well, I have this shopping cart full of them and they need to get to people in *The Land of the Lost.*"

"No problem," assured the Sky.

Suddenly, a ferocious gust of wind blew over the cart, sweeping up all of the flyers. The papers swirled into the air, all the way up to the clouds, and gently rained down like peculiar snowflakes over the entire forest.

"Wow!"

Jai noticed that a single flyer remained floating in mid-air near an unusually dark cloud.

Hmmmm, thought the cloud, who was actually reading the notice. *I remember wanting to be a rainbow once.*

Jai watched the last flyer as it dropped into the forest below.

"Thanks for your help," shouted Jai up to the Sky. "That was amazing!"

"You're welcome," answered the Sky, its enormous voice rumbling across the heavens like distant thunder.

After returning the cart, Jai and the cardinal were about to head out towards the other side of the building when she again noticed the unusual dark cloud. It was now drifting surprisingly low in the sky behind them.

"I wonder what a toaster is," mused the cloud as it floated closer to the door, casting a small round shadow over the building's entrance.

Jai continued to make her way along the side of the building. It seemed to go on for blocks and blocks with no end in sight. It was the most massive warehouse she'd ever seen.

"This place is GIGANTIC!" remarked Jai to the cardinal, who was now sitting on her shoulder. "I wonder..."

She was interrupted by the triumphant sound of a gong ringing from inside *The Bureau*. Instantly, a beautiful and unusually elated rainbow appeared in the Sky. It sparkled gloriously in the sun and, strangely enough, appeared to be carrying a toaster.

Jai and the cardinal walked on, eventually arriving at the rear of *The Bureau of Lost Ideas*. As with the entrance, the back of the building was framed by a perfectly manicured lawn. A rotting sign was perched at the outermost edge of the yard. It read:

THANK YOU FOR
VISITING THE
LAND OF THE LOST.
TRY NOT TO
COME AGAIN.

"No problem!" declared Jai.

Craning her neck, she gazed up at the beam of light from The Leather and The Sun. Meanwhile, the cardinal pecked gingerly at the rotting sign.

"Would you *please* turn into an eagle now and take me back up there?"

The cardinal just cocked his bright red head back and forth, turned into a Leaf and floated gently to the ground.

"Whatever," Jai grumbled.

She gently scooped up the Leaf and put it in her pocket. With her back to the awful forest, she set her gaze towards a series of green, sun-drenched hills—and continued on her way.

CHAPTER 20

Jai had been walking most of the morning. As she reached the top of one of several tall, lime-green hills, she paused.

"What a view!" She exclaimed as she gazed out over a strange and endless variety of fields. Color abounded from every direction. To the left were fields of pink tulips and purple irises. To the right grew fields of white daises and yellow dandelions. But incredibly, there were also fields of sparking crystals and even a field of pure white feathers!

"Hello," greeted a deep voice. Jai spun around to see that the welcome had come from an ancient boulder sitting nearby.

"Hi," replied Jai.

"Would you care to sit down?" offered the boulder.

"Yeah, thanks. That'd be great."

"Well, climb on up."

Jai raced to the top. The Stone exuded a quiet, noble strength.

She and the boulder took an instant liking to one another. They spoke for a long time about many things. She told the boulder about the Water Trees, of her Great Adventure, and stories of her friends at school. The boulder shared with her about what it was like to sit on the earth for a trillion years. They had a lot in common.

After a while, Jai lay down on her back and looked up at the sky. Thousands of feet above, the light from the Leather and the Sun still flickered across the heavens.

"You'll get back up there," assured the boulder. "Don't worry. You won't end up like those other flowers."

"What do you mean? What flowers? And besides, I'm a girl, how could I ever end up like a flower?"

"Not any flower, *those* flowers," answered the boulder.

Jai sat up to inspect the landscape. Everything looked fine as far as she could tell.

"Not the flowers here, Jai. You'll come across them. And when you do, you'll know."

"Know what?"

"They never learn," continued the boulder.

"Learn what?"

"It's simply a shame," continued the boulder.

Just then, the soft pulse of drums returned. But they weren't in the sky as before. They seemed to be pulsing from within the boulder itself.

"Ah, now you are beginning to understand!" noted the ancient stone.

"I am?"

"Indeed," answered the boulder.

The drumming stopped and the two sat together in silence.

After a while, Jai asked, "Um...what *exactly* am I understanding?"

The boulder didn't say a word. It remained perfectly still, as rocks often do, giving her time to consider what she'd heard.

A few moments later, Jai thanked the boulder and continued on her way. A flood of questions swirled through her brain. *What could a flower possibly do that was so terrible? How could there be a drum inside a rock? Why won't my Leaf fly me back up there?* Overwhelmed, she began to feel tired. Her feet started to drag. Soon, she heard a crowd of voices giggling.

"Hello!" sang the throng, "We're over here."

A nearby field of pure white feathers was calling to her. The gathering of plumes quivered softly, stretching lazily over the meadow.

"Would you care to lie down?"

Jai yawned and rubbed her eyes.

"Is it okay?"

"Of course," sang the throng.

"Thanks."

The soft, plush field held her gently and a warm breeze blew across her brow. She soon fell fast asleep.

◇ ◇ ◇ ◇ ◇ ◇

"Excuse me," called a young voice.

Jai found herself sitting near a field of roses, next to a young slender blade of grass. It appeared to be growing right out of a small rock. The little Sprout smiled tenderly, shining softly in the sun.

"Do you live here?" asked the Sprout.

"No, I think I'm dreaming right now," answered Jai, looking

around.

"Oh. Well, I just got here. I was born today."

Jai looked closely at the tender blade of grass. It gazed back at her with soft, curious eyes, marveling at the world around it. The very tip of its blade was still curled slightly, like it had just pushed out of the ground.

"What is that thing?" asked the Sprout, gazing up in astonishment.

"That? Oh, that's the sky."

"It's HUGE!"

"Yeah, you should try walking through it sometime. That's truly amazing."

"You walked through the sky?" The Sprout was in awe.

"Yeah, until I fell off anyway."

"I don't think I'd be able to get up there, being rooted and all."

The young sprout *did* have a point: being human definitely has its advantages. Then again, Jai didn't think she would ever be able to grow out from a rock.

"Will you become a tree one day?" asked Jai.

"I don't think so. I think I'm just a blade of grass."

The Sprout shimmered quietly. It radiated such sweet innocence that Jai couldn't help but smile.

A small bead of morning dew had gathered at its tip. The Sprout was about to take a sip until, glancing at Jai, noticed she looked thirsty.

"Would you like some?"

"You mean, water? I am a little thirsty, but there isn't

enough for both of us."

"Sure there is! Just put out your hand." The Sprout bent over and the bead rolled easily into Jai's palm.

"Thanks! But what about you?" Jai marveled at the generosity of this simple creature.

A tiny bit of dew remained on the tip of the Sprout. "See? I have some too."

Jai licked her palm. Truly, it was the sweetest water she'd ever tasted. Remarkably, even though it was a single drop, her thirst was completely quenched. The Water Trees had talked about this one time. They said even if you don't have much, when you share, there's always enough to go round. As always, they were right.

Jai reached into one of her pockets.

"Are you hungry? I have some nuts."

"No thanks. All I need is water and sun."

Still, Jai wished she could give something in return. Just then, the wind picked up, blowing her hair in all directions. She immediately reached over and cupped her hands around the Sprout, protecting it from the gust until it had passed.

"Thanks!" replied the Sprout, still a bit shaken.

"No problem. Don't you worry about the wind—just keep growing. Once your roots are deeper, that sort of thing won't be a problem." Jai had learned that from Ms. Hanks during a biology class.

The Sprout gazed up at Jai with shy and adoring eyes.

Y'know," it confided truthfully, "I think you're my very first friend."

In fact, the Sprout was correct. The Water Trees had talked about this too. They said that True Friendship is a rare and precious gift; that people can have lots of "friends," but True Friendship is something else altogether. According to the Water Trees, a True Friend is someone you can trust to share what's most important—whether it's a tiny sip of water or the deepest secret. And a True Friend is someone who will be there when you really need them, like when a gust of wind blows by and there's nothing to protect you. It's never a one-way sort of thing.

Captivated by the sky's brilliance, the Sprout continued to watch, marveling at the light that poured forth from The Leather and the Sun.

"So how'd you fall off?"

"Oh that? Well, I was thinking the wrong stuff."

The Sprout looked at Jai, confused.

"I went against some advice a Mosquito gave me," continued Jai.

"Got it." The Sprout made a mental note to pay close attention to what insects have to say.

"So, where's your mom?" asked Jai, looking around for an older blade of grass.

"My mom? She's right here!" The Sprout pointed to the soil. "Where's yours?"

"My mom died."

The Sprout's little jaw dropped.

"She...*died*?"

"Yeah. But she visits me in dreams. She's amazing—you'd really like her. And she's really pretty, too. Wanna see?" Jai reached into her pocket and displayed the picture of herself with her parents. The sprout looked at the photo in awe.

"I can't ever imagine living without my mother." The soil held her firmly, with reassurance she'd never be alone.

"Your dad looks nice too," offered the Sprout.

"Yeah, he is." Jai felt a pang and her shoulders drooped.

"What's wrong?"

"He doesn't know I'm here and I don't want him to worry."

The Sprout smiled. Her eyes grew wide with the excitement of a new idea. "Well maybe your dad saw you walking on the light and he knows you're okay, so he's okay too."

There was something in the way she said it—so open and full of promise—that the heaviness in Jai's heart completely lifted. After all, the Water Trees had said that everything would be all right—even better than that. For the first time, she actually believed it. In that moment, Jai realized she now had two True Friends in her life: Billy and the Sprout.

They talked for hours, sharing secrets, joking around and enjoying each other's company. Eventually, emptied of conversation, they sat in silence. Jai's eyelids grew heavy. Thoroughly content, she began to nod off.

"Do you mind if I rest here?"

"Please do."

Jai curled up next to her friend, and fell fast asleep.

She soon awoke to find herself back in the field of feathers, grateful for the wonderful dream and a brand-new friend.

"Hello," offered a voice.

Amidst the swaying sea of feathers, a single Tulip spoke to her. Its bright orange petals opened into a perfect bloom, smooth as a fresh bar of soap.

"Are you the one trying to get back up there?" asked the flower, pointing to the sky with one of its leaves.

"Yeah, that's me," answered Jai as she stretched and sat up.

"So *you're* the one! I saw you on your way down."

"Hmmmm." That made sense to Jai. After all, the flowers *do* look up at the Sky all day.

"Anyway," continued the tulip, "I have a message for you. It's from the Sky. It didn't want to wake you up while you were in the middle of making a new True Friend. So it asked me to tell you instead."

A message from the Sky? Jai thought, *This must be very important!*

"It is," replied the flower, reading her thoughts.

"Ok, I'm ready. What's the message?"

"To have a calm mind."

"That's it?"

"That's no small thing," noted the Tulip.

Jai stood up, knee-deep in the feathers.

"My mind's pretty calm," she replied, stretching. "Especially now that I'm out of *The Land of the Lost!*"

The tulip shrugged.

"I'm just the messenger."

Jai thanked the flower and the field of feathers and continued heading towards some hills in the distance. As she reached the crest of a hill, a sign abruptly popped out of the ground, right in front of her. Startled, she jumped back and almost rolled down the hill.

Jai stared at the sign. She shrugged, walked around it and kept walking. A few steps later, another sign jutted out from the ground, almost tripping her this time.

Jai scratched her head. The signs had never repeated themselves before. For that matter, they never shot out of the ground like that either. As soon as she walked around the second one, two more signs popped up. The third one was larger than the others, and the fourth was the size of a billboard. The message remained the same—only with larger and larger letters. At the fourth sign, Jai stopped, looked up at the Sky and asked,

"Uh, excuse me. Can you tell me why this happening? And what's a 'false time blow'?"

Silence.

There was nothing to do but continue and climb to the top. Once there, she gasped in awe and delight.

Each field in the distance was aglow—as if dipped in light. In fact, each one was literally soaked in a different shade of sky. In one field, the sky was bright pink, in another—purple, in yet another—orange, and still another—gold. She'd never seen anything so spectacular in all her life.

Eager to know more, Jai raced towards the flower fields. As she came closer, however, her heart sank to her feet— slowing her sprint to a stagger. She couldn't believe the scene before her. The multi-colored sky remained perfect and breathtaking but to her horror, each and every field was decimated. Dead and dying flowers lay smashed everywhere. Scattered amongst them were hundreds of small, cracked rocks. Every single colorful field, all the way to the horizon's edge, had been destroyed.

"What happened here?" whispered Jai. Her shock was interrupted by a voice.

"Will you just look at this place?! I hope you're all satisfied!"

It was a Stem, and a very annoyed one at that. There, on the lowest branch of a nearby tree, it sat shaking its head from side to side in disbelief, inspecting the vast expanse of withered and crushed flowers. The Stem sat next to a tiny easel, canvas and paint set. Apparently, this Stem was a fine artist.

"What a waste!" continued the Stem to the fields of bruised and broken flowers. "I was looking forward to painting a landscape today, not a mangled potpourri! Just look at you!"

"Hey, don't blame us," replied the stones that were strewn all about. "We just happened to land here."

"NOW what am I going to paint?!" continued the Stem. "Do you have any idea how long it took for you to grow here? One minute you're a beautiful garden, and the next, you're compost! What's wrong with you people?! Will you EVER learn?!"

"What happened here?" asked Jai again, not whispering this time.

"An argument over NOTHING!" replied the Stem. "The flowers in the field over there, where the Sky is purple, insisted that *their* Sky was the best. The flowers over there, where the Sky is pink, insisted that *their* Sky was the best. And the flowers over there, where the Sky is orange, insisted that *their* Sky was the best! And then they all got into a huge fight about it!"

Jai noticed hundreds of miniature slingshots strewn on the ground beside the fallen flowers.

"You mean they've been slinging stones at each other?" She had never considered such a thing was even possible.

"You got it," replied the Stem, irate.

Jai scanned the desolated countryside before her. Most of the flowers had already died—struck down by the rocks which now lay beside them. The stones were smeared with decaying petals.

"They all started hurling stones at each other," continued

the Stem. "Some got hit and then others got angry because their friends were getting hurt. Soon everyone was throwing stones, everyone was mad at each other, and everyone was getting hurt."

"But that makes no sense!"

"No it doesn't!" replied the Stem. "But be careful. This sort of thing is contagious."

"I could never hurt a flower!"

"You have a good heart, kid. Even so, you must be careful."

Jai thanked the Stem and began to move on, wading through the carnage, bewildered. Then she noticed two flowers that remained standing. The flowers glared at one another from opposite ends of the field. Walking between them, Jai could feel the hair rise on the back of her neck. Nervous, she picked up her pace then almost tripped when she heard a small voice.

"Jai, is that you?"

There, between heaps of smashed petals, was the Sprout from her dream. The tender blade smiled sweetly, its tip still slightly curled, just as before.

"It's YOU!" exclaimed Jai, overjoyed to be reunited with her new friend. "And look at you! You're still growing, even in the middle of all this!"

The Sprout shuddered with fear as it saw the destruction around it. "What happened?"

"I don't know," Jai answered as she knelt towards her friend. "But I think we need to get you out of here. Everything's ruined."

The Sprout looked at Jai with soft innocent eyes. "But I'm

rooted, remember?"

"Maybe I can transplant you. I'll be super careful, I promise. My dad taught me how. We've done a lot of gardening together."

Jai was determined. She'd do everything she could to help her friend. Even if it meant carrying the tender young blade for the rest of her journey. She stood up and looked around, wondering which way to go.

Just then, two stones sailed through the air from opposite directions. The two remaining flowers had hurled them at each other, each shouting, "The color of OUR sky is the BEST!" Jai and the Sprout happened to be directly between them. She didn't notice, but one of the rocks was speeding right for the back of her head.

In a flash, the Leaf dropped from her pocket, changed into a hawk and swooped up to deflect the shot. Jai heard a horrible cry. Turning around, she saw the bird—lifeless—on the ground. It had been hit. The hawk had morphed back into a Leaf. But it was no longer a beautiful blue. Instead, it had turned to ashen gray and was shriveling around the edges.

"My LEAF!" screamed Jai.

At the same time, the second rock had also landed, striking the little Sprout. Jai turned just in time to see a single drop of dew roll from its curled tip onto the soil.

"NO!" she screamed.

The soil beneath her trembled and wept.

"You killed them!" she shrieked.

Blinded with rage, Jai picked up a rock and frantically

aimed at one flower, then the next. Neither of the blooms would stand a chance. Jai was the best baseball pitcher in the school.

Bzzzzzzzzz!

"Ouch!"

The Mosquito was biting Jai sharply on her pitching arm.

"Jai, STOP!" commanded the Mosquito.

Jai clenched the rock and kept her arm cocked, glaring at the flowers across the way.

"STOP, JAI!" screamed the Mosquito, biting her repeatedly.

Enraged by the impossible sight of her lifeless Water Tree Leaf and her crushed friend, Jai stood ready to attack.

Her arm was now covered in Mosquito bites but she didn't notice. White hot fury pumped through her body, flooding her ears. She no longer heard anything the Mosquito was saying. She HAD to do something... ANYTHING. Those flowers deserved payback for what they had done. Nothing else mattered.

Pulling back her arm, Jai prepared to deliver the hardest fastball pitch of her life. One of the flowers, in the meantime, was also preparing to launch another rock right at Jai.

And that's when it happened. The entire scene froze. Everything around her was drained of color. It reminded her of her dad's faded old black-and-white photos. Even the light from The Leather and The Sun turned gray. It hung heavily in the air like an old cement slab, fading from the Sky.

"WHAT'S HAPPENING?!" screamed Jai, terrified.

"You've fallen into False Time," replied the Mosquito sternly.

"This is False Time? This is a nightmare! GET ME OUT OF

HERE!"

"Then put the rock down, Jai."

"But..."

"PUT IT DOWN!" demanded the Mosquito.

Jai relaxed her arm, but continued to clench the rock in her fist.

"*This* is what it means to forget yourself," said the Mosquito.

"But that flower killed my LEAF! And that other one killed my FRIEND!"

"Stop, Jai! Or you'll never get to *The Land of The Drum*. And you'll never get back home!

"But ..."

"Jai! Listen to me! Revenge will get you nowhere. It's worse than *The Land of the Lost*. Believe me."

"I don't care!"

"Think, Jai! If you throw that rock, you could be killing someone's mother."

Silence filled the air.

"What?"

"Do you really want to kill someone's parent?"

Jai stood speechless amidst fields of crushed flowers and pelted stones, staring at her friend's lifeless body. She'd never considered that those two flowers might have children.

"You shouldn't be involved in this!" continued the Mosquito. "Jai, you've stepped into the middle of a war."

Jai's heart exploded in grief and confusion. Looking up to The Sky, she cried, "Is that what happened to *my* mom? Dad told me she was in a war."

The Sky didn't answer. It simply rained a single tear that landed on a heap of dead flowers.

The Mosquito took a deep breath.

"Yes, Jai, but your mother never threw a rock to begin with. She just happened to be in the way, just like you and your friend."

"So *that's* what Dad meant about Mom being in the wrong place at the wrong time?"

The Sky was silent.

"Yes," answered the Mosquito softly. "Do you really want to do that to someone else?"

Jai fell to her knees, and began to cry. She missed her mom with all her heart.

"How could I do such a thing?"

She released the rock from her hands. It fell to the ground with a soft thud.

The flower that had been reloading its slingshot now stared curiously at Jai. It was shocked that someone on the enemy's side would choose to spare its life. Not knowing what else to do, the flower tossed the rock and the slingshot to the ground. That's when Jai noticed the children. Baby blooms were huddled together, trembling behind their flower parent. They were terrified. Witnessing all of this, the second flower also lowered its slingshot and let it drop to the ground.

All was still.

Jai watched as the color slowly began to return to the landscape. She turned her gaze upward and saw that The Leather and The Sun was regaining its original brilliance. She looked down at The Sprout's small, lifeless body as it lay among the other crushed flowers. It had died.

With great reluctance, she glanced over at the gray Leaf. But then she thought she saw a hint of blue at one of its edges. She ran up to it for a closer look and gasped. Like the nighttime sky emerging, hues of rich vibrant blue swept their way across the entire Leaf.

"It's just like the Water Trees said!" Jai screamed in amazement. "Nothing can hurt you as long as you're allowed to be free!" Soon, the Leaf was good as new. It sat up, morphed into a raven, and flew to perch on Jai's shoulder.

"Thanks for saving my life," Jai said.

The raven cawed softly in return.

The Sprout, however, remained silent. It was gone.

"Beware of False Time," whispered the Mosquito. "The older you get, the easier it is to fall into, if you're not careful. Always read the signs, Jai. Choose to be the bigger person. Try to see the bigger picture. And *just stay calm.*"

Overwhelmed, Jai sat quietly reflecting for a long while. Eventually, she looked up at The Sky and whispered, "How do I do that?"

CHAPTER 21

Ms. Hanks glanced at the clock.

"Okay, Billy, go ahead."

Billy raced to the classroom windows and gazed out at the sky. "Window patrol" had quickly become his favorite school activity.

"It's still there," he announced, peering at the mysterious thread of light that sparkled across the heavens above.

"Hmmmmm," replied Ms. Hanks, deep in thought. "If it's still there tomorrow, we're going on a little field trip."

"REALLY?" exclaimed the class, excited. "To where?"

"The Water Tree Grove."

Everyone looked at one another, bewildered. They all wanted to go, but the idea of an adult being there felt strange and, well, just plain wrong.

"Of course, you don't have to come, I can easily get a substitute and just go by myself."

"NO, WE'LL GO!!!"

"Ms. Hanks?" asked Billy, "How do you know about Water Trees?"

"Oh, I've known them ever since I was three years old."

"*YOU* were *three*?!" blurted Natalie Snoot. It was

impossible for her to conceive of a teacher being anything but...old. She just figured they came that way.

"Believe it or not, Natalie, my cells split and multiply just like everyone else's." Ms. Hanks couldn't help but throw in a reference to their latest biology lesson.

"Ms. Hanks, have you ever seen a Water Tree Leaf?" asked Michael Peabody Smith III.

Seen one? thought Ms. Hanks, *I've done far more than just that!*

"Yes, Michael," answered Ms. Hanks out loud. "I've seen one or two."

She picked up her chalk and began writing the next homework assignment on the chalkboard.

While everyone else grabbed their pencils to copy the assignment, Billy peered deeply at Ms. Hanks as if looking at one of those posters that have a picture of a dolphin or a boat hidden within it. There was something about her that he just could not clearly see. Their teacher had been acting strangely ever since Jai had left on her Great Adventure.

"Hmmmm," muttered Billy to himself. He picked up his pencil and reluctantly got back to work.

CHAPTER 22

Jai looked up at The Sky, hoping for advice on how to stay calm.

No Answer. The heavens were choosing to remain silent. Then she remembered there was a Stem nearby.

"Excuse me."

"Yes..." replied the Stem, who had put away its paint set and was now reading a book about fine art.

"Can you tell me what *The Royal Academy* says about staying calm?"

The Stem paused.

"Now that's a good question."

"I really need to know."

"*The Royal Academy* always encourages experiential learning in matters such as these. So, rather than trying to *explain* this to you, I suggest you experience it directly for yourself."

"Huh?"

"Do you see that field there? The third one from the left?"

"Yes," Jai replied, looking out over a broad swath of smashed flower fields.

"Good. I suggest you head on over to that field. There is someone waiting for you."

"Who?"

"You'll know who, when you get there."

Jai walked through heaps of smashed flowers and scattered stones. She eventually spotted a single flower—a Rose—standing in the distance. It seemed to be glowing.

As Jai approached the unusual bloom, she noticed that it was, indeed, exuding a most remarkable white light. Even amidst all the destruction, the Rose remained peaceful and completely intact; standing quietly, smiling to the sky, her petals stretched open to the sun.

Truly, this was a remarkable flower. She didn't have a single thorn, and her petals were a soft, simple white.

This is the most beautiful rose I have ever seen. Jai thought.

"Why don't you have a slingshot?" Jai asked the Rose as she approached. "Don't you need to protect yourself?"

"Why, nothing can possibly hurt me, Dear," assured the Rose. She spoke in a tone that was at once ancient and wise.

"Really?" Jai asked.

"Absolutely."

"Not even a rock?"

The flower smiled so beautifully that the ground at her stem began to shimmer.

"Please, sit down," invited the Rose.

Jai took a seat next to the mysterious flower, inhaling her soft, pleasing fragrance. The love exuding from the bloom reminded her of the Water Trees. She didn't quite understand how, but it seemed as if this special rose knew everything about her. Jai thought of her mother, and her little friend who had just died.

"The world is rarely fair, Dear," the Rose said, reading her thoughts. "Many have fallen into False Time and others often pay the price. But most important is that you stay centered and never return a mistake with a mistake. Remember this, Dear One. Remember in a world that has forgotten."

Jai didn't see it, but the stones that had been strewn about the fields were listening too. Just by sitting in the presence of this remarkable bloom, everyone felt better.

"Remember?" asked Jai. "Remember what?"

"Remember to respect yourself. Remember that you, and all beings, are a beautiful and *necessary* part of this Universe. It is just as *The Rule Book* says."

"I... uh... I only read the first couple of pages."

The Rose didn't scold her. She simply laughed heartily, as if Jai had just told the best joke ever. "Well, Dear, ALL Instruction Manuals throughout the Universe speak of this. All creatures, including humans, are born with this knowledge. Many quickly forget it, but it is still there, nonetheless, deep within us."

"What is it?" asked Jai, wide-eyed.

"It's simple: You are beautiful and necessary—and the world would never be the same without you."

A wave of joy and peace washed over Jai as the Rose spoke. It reminded her of how she felt while running to The Water Tree Grove after school or while walking under the great Arch of Light at the beginning of her journey.

"What you are feeling at this moment is the truth of who you *really* are," said the Rose. "Now, understand this: To lose a good idea is one thing, but to lose sight of who you truly are is far worse. Respect yourself Jai, and always remember..."

"How do you know my name?"

The Rose simply smiled. "Remember this, Jai. When others act in hurtful ways, know that they have forgotten who *they* are. Don't forget yourself in return. To react in anger only makes things worse. There is a far wiser and safer path to choose."

"What is it?"

The stones rolled quietly closer, not wanting to miss a single word.

"It is to live from the Center Point."

Jai had never heard of a "Center Point" before. Again reading her thoughts, the magnificent bloom continued.

"The Center Point is a place deep inside of you. It has always been there and always will be. Every living thing has this secret place tucked within them. It is available to everyone and simply waits to be discovered."

Jai carefully inspected the front of her shirt, wondering where *her* Center Point might be.

"The Center Point is made of Pure Love and reminds us— with absolute certainty—that we are all connected, no matter what. Know that when you choose to live from the Center Point, you gain great clarity and therefore great power. When you live from the Center Point you become aware of many truths."

"What kind of truths?" Jai asked.

"You learn that you are never really alone, that life is always giving to you, and providing for you—in countless ways."

"So, when my mom comes to me in dreams, is that a Center Point thing?"

"Yes, Jai. Just as it is when you feel happiness for absolutely no reason at all. No one is ever alone. Love is always there, watching over you, over everyone, at all times."

Jai looked out across the fields of dead flowers and all the gruesome destruction surrounding them.

"But then how did *this* happen?" she asked.

"False Time is a state of forgetting. When the mind is finally used as a mirror and not a camera, problems such as these will cease."

"But what does that mean?"

The Rose smiled and stretched its majestic petals towards the sun. "When painful things happen, Jai—and they will, at some point, happen to us all—we are each faced with a choice. If we let that pain freeze in our mind—like taking a picture—the Center Point can get covered up. It is as if one has put a rag over it.

Once that inner place is covered long enough, it becomes easy to forget that it ever existed."

Jai thought about the people she had met in the Land of the Lost and how clueless they had seemed.

"And this is how one falls into False Time, that state of forgetting. Forgetting you are never alone, forgetting that life is constantly giving, and even forgetting your own self. In such a miserable condition, it becomes easy to make mistakes, which leads to sadness for yourself and others."

"Hmmmmm."

"Now, there is another secret of the Universe. A secret meant for one and all. So far, Jai, you have gathered three. This will be the fourth."

At that moment, the soil beneath them, torn open by the battle, let out a sorrowful moan. To Jai's amazement, the Rose bent over in a perfect arch and softly kissed the ground.

The Rose raised its petals to address Jai. "And the fourth secret is this:

Love will always come to restore and renew, no matter what. It is a fact of the Universe."

Jai felt a small tremor as the soil heaved a sigh of relief, reassured it would eventually heal.

"So let your mind be a mirror," continued the Rose, "where nothing is frozen, and love comes freely."

"Thank you." Jai nodded. She paused for a moment. "Can I ask you one more question?"

"Of course," smiled the Rose.

"Well, the Water Trees said that my dad is in False Time. But he would *never* do anything like this. So what does that mean?"

"Your father is a very sweet man, Jai. And False Time can be expressed in many ways. He's simply forgotten that he's connected to something greater than himself."

"So *that's* why he's like that?"

"Yes. But don't worry, Jai. He'll come around. The rag is slowly coming off."

The love exuding from the magnificent Rose was so soothing and pure; Jai *knew* her words were true.

An idea occurred to Jai that she'd never thought of before, that love isn't an emotion really, like having a crush on someone at school. Instead, it's a sort of power. An invisible power that makes anything possible—even walking on light. And when you doubt that power, like listening to clouds, you fall. And when you hurt someone because they hurt you, like the smashed flowers all around her, you fall even farther.

The Rose nodded and continued. "But no matter how many times you fall, Love is always there, simply wanting to be put to good use. And no matter what, Love always welcomes you back."

Jai remained silent for a long while, reflecting.

The Rose smiled while gazing up at the light from The Leather and The Sun. Pointing to the radiance with one of her petals, she added, "Don't just *walk* on it, Dear. *Be* it. Rise to a higher perspective, Jai, and see what's truly going on. Remember, always let Love lead you."

Jai realized at that moment that all the power in the Universe meant nothing if she did not know how to use it. Love might be the greatest power of All Time, but she was still stranded.

"I don't know what I'm doing!" confessed Jai. Overwhelmed, she blurted, "PLEASE HELP ME!"

Now, according to the Water Trees, one of the best things you can ever do is to admit—with all your heart—when you *really and truly* don't know what you're doing and that you *really and truly* need help.

"After all," the Eldest Tree told her one day after school,

"anything is possible. Miracles happen all the time, but they like to be invited properly. It's just good manners."

The Rose beamed a magnificent smile and replied, "All you had to do was ask in the way you just did, Dear."

The Sky, who had been listening to their conversation, was immensely pleased.

Instantly, the Leaf fell from Jai's pocket and morphed into an enormous Eagle. The magnificent bird gripped Jai by the back of her shirt with its powerful talons, and with a few beats of its mighty wings, lifted them both into the sky. Indeed, it was a miracle.

"Whooooooaaaaa!" screamed Jai, as her feet flew through the air.

"You are free to go now, Dear One, for you seek a better way," smiled The Rose.

"Thank youuuuuuuuuuuuuuuuuuuuuuuuuu!!!"

Jai whizzed towards the ethers with the wind whipping wild freedom in her ears. The ferocious pull of the eagle's wings thrust her body through the sky. She'd never felt so light and powerful in her life. As they flew higher, she heard an odd, high-pitched buzzing. Glancing around, she noticed the Mosquito zooming right alongside her.

"This is amazing!" shouted Jai.

"Look down, Jai," instructed the Mosquito.

"What?"

"Look down."

"Huh?"

BZZZZZZZZZ!

"Ouch!"

The Mosquito bit her on the ankle.

"Is that necessary?" shouted Jai, soaring through the heavens, scratching her ankle.

"It is when you don't listen. I said, LOOK DOWN!"

"Oh."

Jai marveled at the world below her and whispered, "I had no idea."

There, high in the sky and the safe grasp of the great eagle's talons, she saw what she could not have seen while still on the ground. A brilliant rainbow arched across the entire region, flooding the defended territories of the warring flowers. A band of orange light illumined one of the fields, a band of purple light covered another, and a pink light yet another. This continued throughout the color spectrum, as the light from a single rainbow bathed each region in a beautiful and unique hue.

"You mean, the sky is different colors down there because it's all just the same rainbow?"

"Um hmmmm," nodded the Mosquito.

"*That's* what they've been fighting over? Which color of the rainbow is best?"

"They can't see it, but yes, that's what they were fighting over," replied the Mosquito. "So be careful, Jai, and don't forget."

"Don't forget *what*?"

"That we're ALL a part of something bigger, something magnificent."

"Like a rainbow?"

"Indeed."

Trying to fathom the enormity of it all, Jai wondered if Ms. Hanks knew anything about this. There'd been no mention of *anything* like it in science class.

The scene below grew smaller and smaller. With a few more swoops of her mighty wings, the Eagle arrived at The Leather and The Sun and gently lowered Jai onto the light. The great bird nodded at Jai and quietly changed back into a Leaf, as if nothing had happened at all.

With great respect, she thoughtfully placed the map in her back pocket.

"Thank you," whispered Jai.

"And *this* time," remarked the Mosquito, "don't stop walking."

"Got it."

"And don't trip on that thing, either."

"What thing?"

"Right over there," noted the Mosquito. There, on the beam of light, sat a simple wooden stick. A soft piece of leather was tied to the top, resembling a small light bulb. The unusual object wasn't there before. Jai was sure of it.

"What *is* that?" asked Jai.

"You're going to *The Land of The Drum*, aren't you?"

"Yeah."

"Well, that's a mallet."

"A mallet?"

"You use it to play The Drum," noted the Mosquito.

"I do?"

"You will."

And with that, the Mosquito zipped off into the Sky.

"Uh, thanks!"

She bent down and picked up the mallet. An oddly familiar pulse resonated from deep within it.

This is a Great Adventure, alright, thought Jai, tucking the mallet into her other back pocket.

The path of light stretched out before her, arching into the unknown. She quickly steadied herself and took a step. At long last, she was back on her way.

CHAPTER 23

According to the Water Trees, the best part about making a huge mistake is being given a second chance. That's how Jai felt as she walked over the world the second time around. The same dark clouds approached her as they had before, but this time, she refused to listen. She kept her vision sharp and her feet steadfast. Thousands of feet above snow-peaked mountains and lush forests, high above dense jungles and meandering rivers, over brilliant blue glaciers and red canyons; Jai sailed above them all.

Soon, the light from The Leather and The Sun began to gently bend towards earth. The ocean below was rough with jagged waves that tossed and collided, churning the sea into an angry foam. As the light continued to arch downwards, she spotted an unusual speck in the distance.

"There it is!"

Her moment of celebration was short-lived, however. As she drew closer to the island, she soon realized the light from The Leather and The Sun ended a few miles from shore. Despite having aimed for the island while on Top of the World, she apparently had missed her mark.

"Of all the times for me to miss, why did it have to be NOW?"

Jai had near perfect pitch—in baseball terms, anyway—she *rarely* missed. As the starting pitcher on her school team, she even struck out the older boys. But she had never aimed for anything across the globe before. It was her first international pitch.

Jai gulped as she eyed the menacing waves below which crashed recklessly into one another with violent slaps.

"NOW WHAT DO I DO?!" she shouted to the Sky.

Thoughts raced furiously through her mind. *I could turn around and go back to the Top of the World, but then I wouldn't be honoring The Signs. What if I ended up in The Land of the Lost again? Ugh, I hate this!*

Just then, the Leaf slipped from her pocket, morphed into a seagull and swooped down to the ocean below, skimming its chaotic surface for fish. Now she was really stuck. She couldn't possibly turn around and leave without her Leaf.

"I'm about to drown, and you've gone FISHING?!"

The sea grew even rougher; it swelled and ebbed as its towering waves and frothy whitecaps crashed together in an explosive mist.

"Jai," called an enormous, infinite voice. It was the Sky.

"I can't swim in that!" screamed Jai. "I'M NOT GONNA MAKE IT!"

"You'll be fine, Jai," assured the endless expanse. "Just find The Center."

"But..."

An invisible ensemble of drums suddenly pulsed through the air. Its rhythm swept through the sky, ushering in a mysterious calm. And in a flash, it was gone.

Her senses clear for the moment, Jai knew there was no turning back. She inched her toes to the edge of the light beam. The waves roared and stirred just below her and the salty mist of the surf stung her nose. The high dive back home was child's play compared to this. And then Jai noticed something amazing. Her pounding heart seemed to match the rhythm of the crashing waves below. She continued to focus her attention on her heartbeat, taking calm deliberate breaths. As her pulse slowed she noticed that a small area of the ocean had also calmed. She had found her Center and her target. Jai took a deep breath, held her nose and jumped!

SPLASH!

The roar of the ocean was instantly muffled and all was dark. A violent swirl pulled Jai deeper into the ocean. She felt crushing pressure in her ears and against her chest. Her air was running out and she did not know which way was up. Just as Jai's mind began to go blurry, she popped up to the surface like a cork, and gasped for air.

"HELP!" she screamed, splashing frantically.

The waves continued to strike as Jai attempted to tread in the choppy sea. Suddenly, an unexpected wave slapped her square in the face causing her to swallow a mouthful of seawater. She choked and coughed as if having swallowed a pound of salt.

"HELP!"

The ocean rocked back and forth, like some large terrifying cradle. She was surrounded by thirty-foot waves, threatening to crest at any moment.

Amidst all the commotion, she hadn't noticed the sound of a motor whirring nearby or the clumsy approach of an unusual flying box careening through the air.

"HEELLLLLLLLPPPPPPP!" cried Jai, flailing hopelessly in the current.

"C'mon," shouted an old man's voice.

She didn't hear it.

"I SAID **C'MON!**" yelled the voice.

Jai glanced up, shocked.

There, hovering—more like wobbling—in the air was the strangest helicopter she'd ever seen. It was constructed from several old wooden planks that had been hammered together into a cube, with four large windows, one on each side. Jai could clearly see an old man inside the contraption, fumbling with the steering wheel. Two propellers whirled awkwardly overhead, powered by a small outboard motor that puttered and coughed from the box's rear.

"I said **C'MON!**" repeated the old man as he tossed over a rope ladder made of dank, gray hemp.

"CLIMB UP!" he shouted.

All the while, the seagull floated playfully nearby, bobbing happily in the perilous sea.

As Jai grabbed the rope, a surge of water ripped it from her hands. Flailing, she reached for it again and missed altogether. Just then, a gargantuan wave barreled towards her. At that terrifying moment, her eyes bulging and stinging with salt—a surprising image popped into Jai's brain. Grelda! The old woman was standing happily next to the Thought-O-Vac. And in that very instant, Jai's mind snapped back into place.

"I didn't have my ears cleaned for nothing!" shouted Jai to the colossal wave prepared to crash upon her. "I'm going to that island NO MATTER WHAT!"

With an extraordinary surge of power, Jai pulled and kicked herself up the rope ladder and into the strange flying box, where she collapsed in a drenched heap. The contraption quickly flew off, barely escaping an angry wave.

"Thanks," offered Jai, panting uncontrollably.

The old man reached over from behind the steering wheel and gently patted her on the shoulder. As she glanced at his hand, she noticed something oddly familiar about it. Before she could give it much thought, her body crumpled in exhaustion. She immediately fell asleep.

"Well, hello there!"

It was Earl, eating another banana.

"Earl! Wow, am I glad to see you!"

Her clothes were dry; Jai knew she was dreaming.

"Hey, I have something to show you." Jai reached into her back pocket and retrieved the mallet.

"Well, what d'ya know." Earl grinned with a glint in his eye.

Jai handed it to him. He placed the tip of the mallet quietly to his heart and smiled before handing it back to her.

"Do you know what this is for?" he asked simply.

"To play The Drum, but I don't really know what that

means."

"Well, seems it's time for you to learn about that now. You see..."

Earl continued talking, but Jai had suddenly become so tired that she couldn't stay awake. Despite her struggles to stay present, she soon fell fast asleep within her dream.

◇ ◇ ◇ ◇ ◇ ◇◇

She woke up in the odd flying machine, still soaked.

"Well, here goes," the old man announced from behind the wheel as the contraption made an ungraceful descent towards the island. Jai closed her eyes and held on. Seconds later the flying box landed on the beach with an abrupt thud.

"Hmmmm, it's good to know that this thing can stop!" he remarked while gazing at the island.

"You've never landed this before?"

"Nope." The old man turned off the engine; it sputtered to an eventual stop.

Jai was shocked when he turned to face her.

"I know you!" she exclaimed.

Indeed, she did. There, sitting at the steering wheel, sat the old man whom she had met in *The Land of the Lost*.

"The name's Marvin."

"Hi Marvin, I'm Jai. But how...?"

The old man handed Jai a towel. "Well, I was thinking about our conversation about flying machines after you left when, believe it or not, a flyer dropped down from the sky!"

He still hadn't shaved, but his eyes had changed—they

now twinkled with gleeful mischief as he spoke. "Anyway, I decided to go to this Bureau place. Good thing I got there when I did—there was a long line of people waiting to get in by the time I left. I had my ears cleaned and was given a drawing of an air-buggy that I had made years and years ago, when I was just a boy."

"Your idea!"

"Yes indeed. I'd forgotten all about that drawing. It was my best one. Anyway, I felt strangely inspired after all that and decided to see if it could actually work. And it does!"

The old man looked around proudly at the awkward contraption, gave one of its boards a hearty slap, and laughed out loud.

"I used the wood from *The Land of the Lost*. Might as well use what's available y'know."

"Makes sense to me," nodded Jai, politely admiring the dreary gray decor.

"And now I'm going to fly around the world! After all, it's never too late for an Adventure."

Jai smiled.

"Y'know, I always wondered what it would be like to fly to Jupiter, but I don't think ole' Doris could make it."

"Doris?"

"My Dear, a Captain must always give his ship—or flying machine—a name." The old man pointed to his steering wheel. In its center was a piece of paper, the back of The Bureau flyer actually, with the name "Doris" scrawled out in very ornate pink cursive letters.

"So Doris and I were out on our maiden flight," continued Marvin, "when I saw something splashing in the ocean up ahead. I decided to investigate. I had no idea it was you. You definitely get around, kid. Well anyway, I'd better be going. There's a world out there to explore!"

"Thanks, Marvin!" Jai gave the old man a hug. "Thank you for everything. And good luck with Doris."

"No. Thank *you*, Jai."

Marvin started up the motor. It hiccupped and coughed, eventually churning into a consistent sputter.

"Hmmm. Looks like I'm still having that problem," noted the old man.

"What's wrong?"

"The gears keep sticking. I need some grease."

Jai thought for a minute. "Hang on, I think I have something."

She reached into her pocket and handed Marvin her stick of Perma-Lip. Marvin applied some of it to the gears and the rough grinding sound disappeared.

"Thanks, kid. Hey, do you want your grease back?"

"Keep it," offered Jai as she hopped off Doris onto the sand. "It's a gift."

Marvin clutched the wheel and gave Jai a sprightly "thumbs up."

"See ya over the vast horizon!"

He hit the throttle and the gray wooden cube wobbled into the air. Jai waved as it flew past a small cluster of dark clouds. She noticed a bumper sticker on the back. It read: *"Don't laugh.*

When's the last time YOU tried to make one of these?"

Soon, the contraption was gone. Jai peered out over the turquoise water, enjoying the soft tropical breeze. The ocean had significantly calmed. The seagull continued to drift happily on the waves as the beam from The Leather and The Sun curved into the sea.

Jai admired its sparkling effulgence for a moment and then thought, *It's time to call it back.*

CHAPTER 24

"Okay everyone, *stay together!*" announced Ms. Hanks.

The entire class stood in a cluster on the playground, getting ready to embark upon their field trip to The Water Tree Grove.

"Billy," called out Ms. Hanks. "Will you check the sky please?"

Billy squinted upwards and saw that, indeed, the brilliant thread of light continued to sparkle over the heavens above.

"Yup. It's still there."

"Very well then. Let's go, class, and NO RUNNING!"

"WAIT!" shouted Billy. "Look up!"

Everyone craned their necks upward. There, before their very eyes, the beam of light began to disappear, like a shooting star in reverse. Within seconds, it was gone.

"What just happened?" exclaimed Billy.

"It disintegrated!" gasped Natalie.

"I bet it got eaten up by the earth's atmosphere," proposed Michael Peabody Smith III.

"No, no," smiled Ms. Hanks. "Nothing of the sort."

"Well then what HAPPENED?" Billy asked impatiently.

Still gazing up, Ms. Hanks simply said, "Well, Jai is back on her way."

"But what does that *mean?*" asked Michael Peabody Smith III.

"It *means* that it's time for math. Everyone, INSIDE!"

"WHAT?!" exclaimed the class in unison.

"But we're supposed to go on a field trip!" whined Natalie.

"Yeah," added Billy. "My parents even signed the form so I could go!"

"Now class, we no longer *need* to go so we *won't* go. And that's THAT!"

Nobody said a word. If anyone ever challenged Ms. Hanks after she uttered those two lethal words—"that's THAT!"—it meant trouble.

The class, with drooping shoulders, trudged back into school while Billy lagged strategically behind. When no one was looking, he squinted at the sky to have a private conversation with the stars.

"Billy!" interrupted Ms. Hanks from the school doors.

"Alright, I'm coming."

CHAPTER 25

Jai faced the beam of light, centered her thoughts and summoned The Leather and The Sun to return to her. As she gazed into the sky, awaiting its approach, a surprising question popped into her mind. It was something that Ms. Hanks had asked during science class one day. While standing by the chalkboard with an elastic in her hand, she said:

"Imagine the world's most gargantuan rubber band. If someone were to stretch it all the way across the globe, almost to the point of breaking, and then release it from one end, how fast do you think it would go?"

Jai soon had her answer. Within seconds of calling back the light, it snapped from the other end of the world and raced through the air like a flaring torpedo, headed straight towards her.

Jai gulped and shouted, "...*THIS FAST!*"

As the enormous flare zoomed closer in, there was only one thing to do—RUN!!!

There, on a small, deserted island, Jai ran like crazy while being chased by a diamond fireball. The seagull watched the spectacle from a safe distance offshore.

Jai sprinted frantically down the beach. The wind had

picked up and was now howling furiously all around her. And then, she tripped. Toppling onto the sand, she crouched into a ball and slammed her eyes shut, expecting the worst.

But nothing happened.

The air became perfectly still.

Slowly opening one of her eyes, Jai peered out and discovered that there, at her feet, sat The Leather and The Sun, waiting happily like an obedient dog. Its beads gradually cooled from blinding white to soft gold. Curious, the seagull flew over and began pecking at the leather with its beak.

"Hey, don't do that!"

The bird looked up in a wisecracking sort of way and transformed into a swan. Its elegant feathers gleamed in the island sun as it returned to the water.

"Well, it's sure good to see you again," whispered Jai to The Leather and The Sun. She placed the Leather over her shoulder and carefully positioned the golden disc over her heart. The seeds sparkled a royal greeting, grateful to be home.

The island had eased into a peaceful silence. Jai stood on the sand for a long time, watching the swan swim spirals in the turquoise sea.

"Jai," called a beautiful voice. "Jai."

"Mom?"

"It's time now," whispered her mother sweetly.

"What do you mean?" Her eyes darted everywhere, hoping to see her mother face-to-face.

"Turn around, Dear."

There, on the sand, sat a drum.

"Mom? Mom, where are you?"

Silence.

Jai peered at the drum for a long time. Structurally, it was simple and strong, a small hollowed-out log with leather stretched over the top and bottom, laced tightly together with thin strips of hide. It rested unassumingly on the sand, exuding a strange and beautiful light—at once, peaceful, ancient and strong.

The swan glided out of the water and waddled over to Jai, nuzzling her towards the drum with its beak.

"Am I supposed to play it?"

The swan slowly nodded before morphing back to a Leaf. While tucking the Leaf into her back pocket, she whispered, "Okay, but I don't really know how to do this."

Jai approached the drum. The top was perfectly round; its small wooden body had been shaved and sanded with meticulous care.

Jai timidly picked up the drum. Somehow it felt more like a person than an object. Simple, kind and wise—it reminded her of Earl. She remembered the mallet, retrieved it from her other pocket, glanced up at the Sky and whispered, "OK, here goes."

Jai took a deep breath and slowly struck the head of the drum with the mallet. But as she played, she realized that the drum had a song that *it* wanted to play for *her.*

The drum sang a simple song of innocence and connection and how all things fit together. Jai had never heard such a song before. It sang of how the stars all sing together and how all beings are united, whether they know it or not.

It sang about beauty and balance, and how everything is a necessary part of the Universe—just like the Rose had said. The song didn't have any words, but it said everything. And then it stopped.

Jai stood on the sand, holding the drum, astounded.

Then, suddenly, without warning, the entire Sky filled with rhythm. Drums were playing from everywhere, although Jai couldn't see them. She closed her eyes as the pulses swirled and danced all around her. Everywhere, braided rhythms soared through the air—one within the other, merging into the next— and Jai saw, with closed eyes, everything dancing together: all colors of people, all plants, animals, rocks, planets, stars, everything, and even everything beyond *that*. All things danced together as the drums played on and on. Streams of music traced the paths of galaxies, and together they spiraled throughout the heavens, splashing endless realms of light and color as the drums grew louder and louder. And then, in an instant, the music vanished.

Jai opened her eyes.

She was no longer on the beach. She now stood directly under the second Great Arch of Light at the opposite end of the map—exactly where the Eldest Water Tree had told her to go.

CHAPTER 26

According to the Water Trees, the word "mystery" is a truly beautiful and useful term, especially when remarkable things happen that you just can't explain, no matter how hard you try. For Jai, it was an utter mystery how she ended up at The Great Arch of Light.

Dumbfounded, she stepped out from the gateway onto soft, warm earth. A clear stream trickled near her feet, winding its way to a canyon nearby. Massive rock walls, red and smooth as skin, stood in majestic silence. She saw small rounded plants, and shining trees with speckled bases. The entire place was infused with a power she'd never experienced before.

Jai took a few short steps and stopped, remaining perfectly still, her jaw agape.

"You have traveled far," uttered a male voice.

A Man was standing in front of one of the canyon walls. His eyes and hair were the color of raven's wings. Immensely gentle and kind, his rounded face looked oddly familiar. Jai wondered if maybe they had met in a dream. She liked him immediately. His presence was as peaceful and extraordinary as the canyon itself.

Not knowing what to say, she gently placed The Drum on

the ground and waved hello.

The Man slowly nodded back.

"Hi, I'm Jai," she offered at last.

"Hello, Jai." The Man smiled.

"What's your name?"

"You wouldn't be able to pronounce it," chuckled the Man gently.

"Oh."

"That doesn't matter, though. That's not why you are here."

Jai marveled at the magnificent person before her. His leather garment was the exact same color as her drum, his skin the color of the earth itself. He wore a brilliant blue pendant over his heart.

"Is this *The Land of The Drum*?" she asked innocently.

"Yes."

"It's beautiful here."

"Yes, it is." He wasted no time in formalities. "Now, on your journey, you've seen what brings you closer to your heart, and you've seen what takes you away from it."

"Yeah, I fell off the light at one point." Jai felt like she could tell him anything.

"Yes, but you got back up there. We all fall sometimes, Jai. It is what we do after we fall that matters most."

As she listened, the Leaf slipped from her pocket and morphed into an enormous eagle. The great bird swooped over to the Man and perched on his shoulder. He smiled and continued.

"That's quite a drum you have there."

"Thanks!"

"It was made especially for you, Jai, and will help you to tune your ears."

"Tune my ears?"

"Indeed," nodded the Man.

"I had them cleaned recently. I didn't know I could tune them."

The Man smiled, remaining still for a good while. Jai felt oddly comforted by the silence between them—it was rich and reassuring in a way that she didn't quite understand. Eventually, the Man continued.

"There is an inner music, Jai. Not only music that you can play out loud, but music that you, and all of us—all beings—are naturally a part of, without even trying. Everyone and everything has music hidden deep inside them. But to hear it, one's ears must be properly tuned."

Jai was confused. She looked around to see if a nearby Stem was available to help explain. No such luck.

"It is simple, Jai," continued the Man. "Everyone has a song inside of them, a song that is magnificent and unique. Some are aware of this truth. Others are not. But it's always there, just the same. And when these songs come together, it is truly a beautiful thing to behold."

Jai nodded, listening intently.

"Now, you have questions about the drums you have heard—in the Sky, in the boulder, before you jumped into the ocean."

"Yeah. What WAS that?"

"All of these things were showing you that there is a rhythm. A rhythm that sings deep inside each of us. A heartbeat that connects us all. Music is everywhere, Jai—it lives in everything and everyone. It never stops and only brings good things. Just tune your ears and you can easily hear this, whenever you want."

"But how do I do that?"

"The Drum will help you," answered the Man. "It will help you to be centered in your heart. For it is meant to live from your heart, act from your heart, and make decisions from your heart. The Drum will teach you. It is important that you know who you are, live in harmony with your fellow beings and honor the heartbeat—the inner song—in all life."

Jai thought for a moment. Even with all she'd been shown, there was still so much more to learn.

"Can I ask you a question?"

"Yes," replied The Man simply.

"There's this bully in school named Dax Googan. He's not a fellow being. He's a creep! How am I supposed to live in harmony with *him*?"

The Man laughed out loud.

"It's possible for a fellow being to commit wrong actions, Jai. It's also important to stand up to bullies and to defend those who are picked on, for that is part of what it means to live from your heart. And understand this: bullies are simply those who are lost in False Time. So just be glad."

"Glad?"

"Glad that you're no longer trapped in such misery. You yourself now know what it's like."

Jai shuddered recalling her fall into False Time.

"Wisdom is often born off the heels of mistakes," continued the Man. "Now that you know, you will see things more clearly. This will make more sense over time.

"When you play the Drum, you'll see how things *really* work. Put your hand to your heart, Jai. Listen to the Drum within you."

Jai closed her eyes and felt her heart pulse into her fingers—a strong, steady beat that had been singing all along.

She thought back to the sounds at The Water Tree Grove, where nature's orchestra played spontaneously every day. She'd lie on the grass and simply listen; thoroughly enjoying the endless tapestry of singing birds, crickets, breezes, gurgling streams, and the soft rustling of animals who came and went as they pleased. Somehow *all* these things fit together into a huge unending symphony. But it had never occurred to her that her very own heartbeat was part of all that, keeping time with nature herself.

"What you've heard thus far is only the beginning. Tune your ears, Jai, the entire Universe waits for one and all. Listen and you will hear—just like it says on page nine of *The Rule Book*."

"I, uh, only read the opening pages actually."

The Man's eyes sparkled with laughter. "You've done well for not knowing the rules!"

"Well, I've had a lot of help."

"It's always good to acknowledge that," replied the Man. "On page nine, it simply states: 'What you seek is within you.'"

Still perched on the Man's shoulder, the eagle nodded majestically with fierce, sharp eyes.

"So, be free, Jai. When you play the drum, let it sing to you and teach you. And as you learn, share this good fortune with others. Deep down, we all yearn to remember, to remember our very own song. This inner music never goes away. It simply waits for us. And even if *we* forget at times, the *music* always remembers."

"Remembers what?"

"That we are all beautiful. And that each and every one of us is a necessary part of a much bigger song."

The Man paused briefly before adding, "And now, it is time for you to go."

"Go? But I just got here!" protested Jai. She didn't want to leave.

"You've gotten what you've come here for. It is now for you to take this place with you in your heart—and go."

"But—"

"The more you live it, the more it will become a part of you."

"A part of me? Like repairing The Leather and The Sun?"

"Like repairing The Leather and The Sun. Only for this, you don't need a needle and thread."

"Hmmmm."

"Take the Drum with you and share its joy with many."

"But, why can't I stay?"

"Because you have a job to do."

"I do?"

"We all do, Jai. And nothing is complete until we each do our part."

"Oh."

"And don't worry. We'll meet again—just like it says in *The Rule Book* on page ten."

And with that, the magnificent man disappeared. Flickering specks of bright blue light danced in the air where he once stood. For years, Jai had seen those lights in dreams.

"But I only read the first couple of pages!"

It was too late. The Man was gone.

"Hello?" Jai called out again to him, only to hear her voice echo throughout the canyon. The eagle was gliding in circles high overhead.

"Ugh! Is this *really* the way to end a Great Adventure?" Jai moaned. She stood in silence, still hoping he'd return. Eventually, she heard a voice.

"Don't worry." The words thundered in a booming yet soothing tone. It was the Sky. "Next time, just read more."

Some things really *are* a mystery.

Jai's mood brightened and she realized it really was time for her to go. Remembering to offer a gift, she knelt to the ground next to her drum and remained quiet for some time. Eventually, she whispered, "I want to thank you. I promise to live from my heart and, uh, not to fall off the light on my way back."

"Thank you," replied the Canyon. "Truly, that is a

wonderful gift."

Jai paused once more, took a deep breath and then softly whispered, "Goodbye."

"Goodbye," echoed the Canyon.

And just then, she got it. Every ending is a new beginning—like flowing water in a stream. It might look the same, but the water is constantly changing. It's never the same water twice. And so it is, that Great Adventures never really end. There are always new ones waiting to be explored—every day.

She carefully removed The Leather and The Sun and placed it on the ground. Yet she had no idea of where to aim it. Looking up at the Sky, she asked, "Excuse me, but I can't see The Water Tree Grove from here. Would you point me in the right direction?"

"See it in your mind," answered the Sky, in an infinite sort of way.

"Thanks."

Jai closed her eyes and saw The Water Tree Grove in her mind. She was delighted to see the Eldest Water Tree smiling directly at her, its soft blue bark rippling in the breeze. She touched the beaded disc on The Leather and The Sun. It blazed across the world, a magnificent sparkling bridge through the Sky.

Opening her eyes, she noticed that the eagle, high above, was now heading straight for The Water Tree Grove, to herald her return.

With the Drum under her arm and the mallet tucked in her back pocket, Jai hopped onto the light.

Wait'll Billy and everybody hears about this! thought Jai as she glided homeward across the Sky.

It was a bright and cloudless morning in Jai's hometown. Her father paused as he walked to his car. Oddly, drums could be heard in the eastern sky.

With a nod of approval from Ms. Hanks, Jai's classmates rushed to the window of their classroom.

And all of the Water Trees cheered from the Grove.

Jai was coming home.

EPILOGUE

Jai's return was a great and grand celebration. Billy and all of her friends were waiting for her at The Water Tree Grove. Everyone knew to be there. After all, the Water Trees know everything.

After the gala, Jai headed towards her house. Even though she couldn't wait to see her father, her stomach flipped with every step. What if he was mad at her or, worse yet, sick with worry?

Her thoughts were interrupted, however, by the surprising sight of a man perched happily on a chair in a nearby meadow. His lanky back towards her, the man's arms flailed with joyous abandon as he painted colorful swirls onto a large canvas. She loved the vibrant spirals that poured from his painting. They reminded her of the first time she played her Drum. Jai's heart danced with joy as she gazed at the familiar beauty. But nothing could have prepared her for what came next.

Hearing her footsteps from behind, the man turned around.

"Dad!....DAD?!!!"

Before she could say another word, Jai's father jumped to

his feet, dropped his paintbrush, and ran over to his daughter.

"But...what...how..."

Jai's words, or her attempt at them anyway, were muffled in his shirt, lost in their embrace. Eventually they spoke.

"We have a lot to catch up on, young lady!"

"You start, Dad!"

The two sat down together in the grass.

"Well, on the day that you left, your teacher Ms. Hanks came to the house for a visit."

"She DID?!"

"Yes indeed and she told me that you were on a Great Adventure. That's when I remembered. Ya'know, when I was a kid, I tried pulling off one of those Water Tree Leaves. I'd forgotten all about it."

"You didn't try hard enough, Dad. You have to really _mean_ it."

Her father thought a moment and nodded.

"So then what happened?"

"Well, Ms. Hanks came over every day after school to give me a progress report."

"What???!"

"Then one afternoon, she asked me to come with her to the Water Tree Grove."

"YOU went to the GROVE?!"

"Well, I didn't want to. Honestly, I thought it was all nonsense. But I was so worried about you, I couldn't sleep. You know, I'd completely forgotten that the Trees can talk! They told me you'd be coming home. I held on to that thought for dear life."

"Sorry to make you worry, Dad. But I *had* to go. I was trying to tell you. Mom came to me in that dream...."

She looked at her father, expecting him to not believe her. He remained quiet. Eventually he spoke.

"Jai?"

"Yeah Dad?"

"I...I had the most remarkable dream about your mother while you were away."

"You DID?!"

"She told me that I should start painting. I love it!" exclaimed her Dad, nodding towards the canvas. "I used to paint when I was a kid, Jai. I had forgotten all about that too. Your Mom also told me that I need to get my ears cleaned. She said that you'd know how to help me with that part."

Jai looked at her father compassionately. She smiled at him with a depth and kindness he'd never seen in her before.

"We all need to have our ears cleaned every once in a while," was all she said.

That night, after dinner, Jai introduced her father to her Leaf. And even though he marveled at its velvety blue magnificence, he was quick to establish some rules about it not being allowed to fly all over the place while in the house. Instead, he agreed to let Jai keep her bedroom window open. That way, the Leaf would always be free to come and go as it pleased. Jai and her Leaf were very happy with this arrangement.

The following day at class, Jai was greeted with an

enormous "WELCOME BACK" banner that stretched across the entire chalkboard. A streak of sparkling silver glitter was glued across the top—an attempted replica of The Light from The Leather and The Sun.

"Welcome back, Jai!" announced Ms. Hanks, with an exuberant smile. "In honor of your return, we will begin with Show-and-Tell. You get to go first."

"Wooo hoooo!" Billy was thrilled. As always, he was sitting right behind Jai. He quickly scribbled a note and slid it to her: "Now THIS is the way to start class!"

Jai smiled, got up from her desk and walked to the front, carrying a cloth bag. Everyone watched in eager silence as she retrieved her Drum and mallet. The Drum glowed softly in her hands, glad to be meeting new friends. The entire class gasped in amazement.

"Here's a song I learned while I was away," offered Jai simply

She introduced the beat slowly—a gentle, steady pulse that held the entire classroom as if in a golden bowl filled with light. Soothing rhythms circled and danced all around. Birds gathered outside the classroom windows, tilting their beaks; even the insects listened in. Clouds came closer. Trees swayed gently. As the Drumbeat grew in strength, teachers put down their chalk and classrooms grew silent. For a moment, the entire school was perfectly still as Jai and The Drum sang to all—of mystery, harmony, beauty and triumph. When the song was over, Jai quietly placed the mallet and Drum into the bag.

"Thank you, Jai," said Ms. Hanks softly. "That was truly

beautiful." Turning quickly towards the chalkboard, she wiped a single happy tear from her eye. Turning back around, she continued. "Now, who wants to go next?"

Natalie Snoot had planned to show off her new eyelash curler, but she reconsidered, deciding to save it for another day. In fact, no one else raised their hand—a first in Show-and-Tell history.

Jai returned to her desk. On her way, she cast a special glance at Billy, secret code for: "We'll talk about all this with The Water Trees after school!" Billy winked in return, promising himself to be especially well-behaved so he wouldn't get in trouble and be late.

But instead, it wasn't Billy who would be staying late that day.

As soon as she sat down, Ms. Hanks announced, "Jai, come see me after school!"

"Wow, she's in trouble *already*?" Billy was impressed.

"And *no* peeking from outside the window!" instructed Ms. Hanks, knowing that everyone would want to spy on their conversation.

While the entire room continued to reverberate with excitement, Ms. Hanks firmly adhered to her lesson plan for the remainder of the morning. Eventually, the final bell rang and it was time for lunch. Everyone piled out into the cafeteria.

Dax Googan was up to his old tricks. He was taunting a younger boy, telling him to hand over his desert. The boy refused and Dax was getting ready to punch him.

Normally, Jai would have shouted him down, insisting that

he stop or she'd clobber him (and of course, she could). But this was the first time she'd seen him since her return. She watched him from across the room—as if inspecting something for the first time.

About to deliver a blasting punch, Dax was suddenly distracted. With his fist clenched, his arm poised, he turned his head towards her and froze. Jai kept looking into him—she *knew* that place. How could he have landed in something as awful as False Time? What had happened to him?

Suddenly feeling naked, Dax dropped his arm.

"Forget it," was all he said, and he quickly pushed his way out of the room.

Everyone was quiet.

"What was THAT?" asked Billy, wide eyed.

"We'll talk about it at the Grove," whispered Jai.

The rest of the day was school as usual, and when the final bell rang, Jai stayed in her chair as instructed. No one hid under the classroom window outside. Not even Billy, who went straight to the Grove with his soccer ball.

Only Jai and Ms. Hanks remained. The room was filled with a peculiar silence that is particular to classrooms after school, a sort of dull roar following a full day of activity. Other than the clock that seemed to tick louder than usual from its perch above the chalkboard, the room was completely still.

Jai took a deep breath and walked up to Ms. Hanks, who, as usual, was seated at her desk, grading homework with her bright red pencil.

"Well?" smiled Ms. Hanks, looking up from her papers. Her

eyebrow arched in soft amusement.

"Yes, Ms. Hanks?" asked Jai, still confused.

"Is there something you want to ask me, Jai?"

Well, there were a *million* things that Jai wanted to ask in that moment—about her Dad, about the daily "progress reports." How did Ms. Hanks know these things?! Yet all of Jai's questions seemed to roll up into a wordless ball.

"It's just like *The Rule Book* says on page eleven," continued Ms. Hanks.

"You know about that TOO?!!!"

"Let me guess. You didn't get up to page eleven, now did you?" Ms. Hanks spoke in a teacher sort of way.

"How could she POSSIBLY know that?!" Jai thought to herself.

"Well Jai, on page eleven it clearly states: 'Even after you've been on a Great Adventure, there's always more to learn.'"

Jai nodded in stunned and silent agreement. Ms. Hanks waited patiently for her to reply. Nothing. Eventually, Jai was able to manage an audible *"gulp"*—but that was about it. Satisfied with the effort, Ms. Hanks continued.

"I think it's time to show you something."

Putting down her red pencil, Ms. Hanks reached for the handle of the bottom left drawer of her desk. It had been left ajar, and was exuding a soft blue light that sparkled slightly.

In Great Adventure terms, this *is* The End. Because, after all, true endings really *do* herald new Beginnings. That's just the Water Tree way—just like it says in *The Rule Book* on page twelve.

Jai peered curiously as Ms. Hanks slowly opened the drawer. She gasped in wonder and delight, Indeed, it was an Astonishing New Beginning.

ACKNOWLEDGMENTS

"We are indebted to the world and to all the beings in it, all of which have nourished us, and brought us to our current state."

~ Amma

And so, I'd like to thank each and every experience of success and failure in my life thus far that has led to the creation of this book. Since that would require another several hundred pages, I'll narrow it down here to a few essential honorable mentions.

First and foremost, I'd like to thank Amma for Her boundless Love and Inspiration on every possible level. This book would never have been possible otherwise. To all of my solo journeys throughout the southwestern desert of the US— the animals, plants, rocks, open sky, seen and unseen sparkling beings who have come my way, I am eternally grateful.

So many thanks to:

Dear friends—John Morse, Jane Goodall, Ellen Papadeas, Andrea Israel, Marsia Shuron Harris, Linda Sherman, Krena Horowitz, Sally Anderson, Emily B. Thomas, Heather Carbine, Kelly Manjula Koza, Arpana Grace Warren, Iswari Cynthia Grace, Angie Shyr, Tangela Stanley, Kim Mackey Pacheco, Julie Woods, Jay Gregory, Suzanna Sifter, Consuelo Candelaria-Barry, Sam Barry, Liam Barry, Rajee Atree, Asha Pillai, Kamini Avril Tucker, Gynux and Sreekutty Nair—for taking the time to pour through whichever version of the manuscript I sent to you at the time, and offering your honest feedback and edits. Special thanks to editor Bart Schull for smashing what I thought was "THE final draft" into smithereens-- ultimately helping me to become a far better writer. Thank you, Bart, for hours and hours of conversation, invigorating debates and patient mentoring. The heart and soul of this book would not shine nearly as brightly without your friendship, talent and expertise. To my beautiful partner Deb Tyler, thank you for your loving heart, eagerness to troubleshoot (suggesting that the book conclude with an epilogue and not an entire chapter was brilliant!), and making some of the best soup in the universe.

To Arch Apolar, thank you for the magnificent artwork. You are a gleaming constellation of imagination and craft. To Chris Nelson, thank you for your extraordinary generosity and expertise in formatting and everything else required to manifest this into a real book.

I'd also like to thank the many notebooks, pens and laptops that I used to bring this story to life.

To all artists everywhere, thank you for taking the time, making the sacrifices and having the courage to develop and share your gifts with the world.

Lastly, I would like to thank you, the reader. This book is meant for you. It brings me immense joy to know that you now have it.

Photo by Jeanine Vitali

ABOUT THE AUTHOR

Throughout her award-winning career, author/composer/ producer Ruth Mendelson's deepest commitment is to bring love, compassion and positive change to children of all ages via a wide range of creative projects and programs.

A New York Times Critics' Pick and Emmy nominee, Ruth has been composing scores for film, HBO, National Geographic, Discovery Channel, Disney, Animal Planet, The Learning Channel, PBS, CBS, and NBC (among others), as well as creating innovative multi-media "surround-scapes" for over 20 years. She was the first woman in the history of Berklee College of Music (Boston, MA) to teach in the Film Scoring Department, where she designs and teaches master classes in documentary and dramatic scoring.

An active studio musician, Ruth has been featured playing a number of instruments in a wide variety of genres with artists in LA, New York, Boston, Europe and India. She is also a guest lecturer and music director. She has performed at the United Nations, in Geneva, Switzerland, as bassist for the One Human Family Gospel Choir, and is currently collaborating with renowned primatologist Dr. Jane Goodall on a variety of youth empowerment and environmental projects. Ruth is founder and president of Eagle Vision Initiatives, a non-profit organization dedicated to serving society through communications and the arts. Eagle Vision's premier initiative, the WELL WISHES Project, is now establishing unprecedented lines of communication and resources between the world's youth.

To learn more about Ruth, please visit: ruthmendelson.com.

Made in the USA
Las Vegas, NV
09 December 2020